The

John

Simmons

Short

Fiction

Award

University of

Iowa Press

Iowa City

Barbara Hamby

Lester

Higata's

20th

Century

1-6697

University of Iowa Press, Iowa City 52242
Copyright © 2010 by Barbara Hamby

www.uiowapress.org

Printed in the United States of America

The University of Iowa Press is a member of Green Press
Initiative and is committed to preserving natural resources.

Printed on acid-free paper

Library of Congress Cataloging-in-Publication Data
Hamby, Barbara, 1952–
Lester Higata's 20th century / Barbara Hamby.
    p.   cm.—(The John Simmons short fiction award)
ISBN-13: 978-1-58729-918-6 (pbk.)
ISBN-10: 1-58729-918-6 (pbk.)
ISBN-13: 978-1-58729-942-1 (ebook)
ISBN-10: 1-58729-942-9 (ebook)
I. Title.
PS3558.A4216L47 2010
813'.54—dc22   2010007647

For

Clarencena Carpenter Hamby,

the best mother a girl ever had

Contents

ACKNOWLEDGMENTS

If you're lucky you have maybe one or two magical things happen to you in a lifetime. Growing up in Hawai'i was such a piece of luck for me, and it is a light I carry within me always.

I have so many people to thank I hardly know where to begin, so I'll start at the beginning with Harriet Nichiguchi, my fifth-grade teacher at Waianae Elementary School, who took a *haole* girl from Virginia and introduced her to another world. Other treasured teachers are Joyce Wong and Willis Moore at Hawai'i Baptist Academy and Elizabeth Koch at Radford High, who introduced me to Kafka. More recently I owe a huge debt to my colleague at Florida State University, Robert Olen Butler, who allowed me to sit in on his graduate workshop. Not only is he a marvelous writer but a generous teacher and friend.

I would also like to thank Bamboo Ridge Press for all their support. Eric Chock, Darrell H. Y. Lum, Joy Kobyashi-Cintrón, Wing Tek Lum, and everyone involved with the press and *Bamboo Ridge* magazine are doing noble work in the world of literature and giving voices to those who need to be heard. I especially want to thank Normie Salvador for his advice on all things local and especially all things pidgin. Any mistakes are mine, and there would be many more without his painstaking reading of the manuscript of this book.

I'd also like to thank the other editors who first published these stories. Residencies at the MacDowell Colony and the Lillian E. Smith Center for the Creative Arts gave me acres of time to work.

Other people who have either read separate stories or the entire manuscript are Amy Watanabe, Colleen Knudsen, and Benjamin and Elsie Yanagida Knudsen. I owe you big time. Thank you Jane Takaki and Grace Hiroda for talking story with me. And a special thanks to the memory of Helen Tamashiro and Grace Kawai, who were so patient with my questions.

The character of Lester Higata has been a part of me for so long that I sometimes forget he is not a real person. His name, though Japanese, is not one heard in Hawai'i, but I chose it for that reason, to free me to give him the life he insisted was his. In Lester I wanted to pay tribute the 100th Infantry Battalion and the 442nd Regimental Combat team, both comprised of Japanese

American soldiers who fought so bravely in World War II. One book especially was helpful in writing Lester's story—*Japanese Eyes, American Heart*, an oral history of these men. I've used some details of their experiences to create Lester's war. I hope I've done them justice.

In many ways this book is a love letter to Hawai'i and to family. We have many families as we move through our lives, but we start with one, and I want to thank my family, especially my sister Quincie, who read this manuscript and gave me encouragement when I needed it. She has a big heart and an artistic soul. My brothers, Tommy and Jeff, told me many stories that have resurfaced in different forms in these pages. I owe a special debt to my late father, Tom Hamby, who for many years would send a weekly envelopes of cuttings from the *Honolulu Advertiser*, especially the Island Life section, so I could keep abreast of what was going on in my mainland exile. He also told many stories of his service during World War II that informed the narrative of this book.

I owe my husband, David Kirby, a debt I can never repay for his careful readings of these stories and the ones that didn't make it into the final manuscript. Without his daily love and beautiful spirit my life would not be such a moveable feast. But above all I would like to thank my mother, Clara Hamby, not only for her love and encouragement but also for her deep love of the islands. If not for her, this book would not exist, and so I dedicate it to her with much aloha and the deepest gratitude for my life, her faith, and the way she has always tossed words around and made them spin and laugh and do cartwheels on the lawn.

The stories in this collection were first published in the following magazines: "Katherine Higata and the Four Japanese Ladies" in *Bamboo Ridge*; "Lani Dances the Zombie Hula in LA" in *Five Points*; "Invasion of the *Haoles*" in *Harvard Review*; "The Thirty Names of Kū" in *Lo-Ball*; "Mr. Manago's Mango Trees" in *Mississippi Review*; "Iniki Chicken" in *Southwest Review*; "Linda Higata's Room" (as "Lipona Street") and "Lester Higata and the Orchid of Divine Retribution" in *Shenandoah*; "Lester Higata's String Theory Paradise" in *TriQuarterly*.

*Lester
Higata's
20th
Century*

Lester Higata's String Theory Paradise 1999

Lester Higata knew his life was about to end when he walked out on the lanai behind his house in Makiki and saw his long-dead father sitting in a lawn chair near the little greenhouse where Lester kept his orchids. A butter-yellow *Laelia* was in bloom, its flowers like a scattering of exotic dragonflies taking off in flight. *I'll bring it in the house later,* Lester thought, *for the dining room table or maybe the dresser in the bedroom.* On the middle row was a white *Phalaenopsis* he could take to church on Sunday. Its bloom was cascading over his father's head like a fancy hat.

Minoru Higata looked pretty good for someone who'd been dead almost sixty years. His hair was black and thick, and he was wearing his favorite plaid cotton shirt just as he had the last time Lester saw him. It was right after Pearl Harbor, and Lester was leaving Hawai'i for basic training in the mainland. Lester closed his eyes, but when he opened them his father was still there, nodding to the chair beside him as if to say, "Sit down, Lester. I want to talk to you."

Maybe I'm dead already, Lester thought, but the sky was still blue, though dark clouds were banking over the mountains, and a cool breeze was rustling through the trees. He hadn't slept well the night before, so maybe he was asleep and dreaming. Whatever it was, he sat down next to his father and said, "Hi, Dad."

"Lester," his father said. "Why did you choose that name?" His feet were bare, and the calluses on the bottoms were thick, almost like the soles of a pair of shoes.

"A lot of the boys in the army chose *haole* names," said Lester, though he hadn't been a boy since he went away to war. "It made us more American. It was kind of dicey for us since we were fighting the Japanese."

"Why *Lester*?"

"Oh, there were a lot of reasons," Lester said, looking at his father's skin, which was glowing as if he had a 100-watt bulb instead of a brain inside his skull.

"Give me two," Minoru Higata said, tilting his head. Lester had forgotten how his father used to do this when he was zeroing in on some lie Lester had told.

"Lester Young was a hero of mine," Lester said. "I used to listen to his records at my friend Tak's house. He played a sweet sax."

"And . . ."

The word reverberated in the morning air like one of the bombs the Germans lobbed at his battalion as they made their way to Rome during the war.

Lester gave up. He never could lie to his father for long.

"I thought it was funny because Mom couldn't say the L." Lester was waiting for his father to come down hard on him, but hearing his mother say "Resta" never stopped being hilarious, especially when she was doing her imitation of Medusa.

"It *was* funny," his father said, laughing and hitting his knees with open hands.

Okay, Lester knew he was dead. It was never all right for a

Japanese boy to make fun of his mother, no matter how much of a gorgon she was.

"Where's Mom?" he asked his father.

Minoru Higata turned away, inspecting the back of his rough hand. "Who knows," he said. "Maybe she's in some kind of detention camp for people who had nasty dispositions."

"You're kidding," said Lester. This was not the afterlife the Christian church had led him to expect. Buddhist either, for that matter.

"Yes, I'm kidding. I haven't seen her. The afterlife isn't as organized as you might think. People go their own ways." He jumped up and went into Lester's greenhouse, picked up a couple of pots, sniffed them, and turned them in his hand.

"It's been thirty years since she died, and you haven't run into her once?"

"We're not locked into three dimensions," Minoru Higata said without turning to face his son. "Time is porous when you don't have a body. I saw her once, but I was in no hurry to jump back into that vat of poison. Sorry to be so hard, but she was not an easy woman to live with. You were smart not to move in with her when you married that nice *haole* girl."

"I never considered it," Lester said and would have crossed himself if he'd been a Catholic.

"How many orchids do you have in here?" his father asked. He was squatting now in the middle of the greenhouse, looking up at the roof, which was made of Plexiglass to let the light through to the plants.

"I don't know," said Lester. He wanted to move closer to his father, but he seemed to be stuck in his chair. "Maybe fifty or sixty."

"Sixty-four," said his father, jumping up from a full squat. "Exactly." He was smiling like a kid who'd mastered tying his shoes or his seven-times table. "Hawai'i has changed since I was here last."

"Worse in some ways," said Lester, thinking about all the cement covering O'ahu. He could hear the faint roar of Honolulu even here in the cool foothills of Tantalus.

"Better, too," said his father. "You didn't have to work in the cane fields."

"You're right about that, but I had to see tightfisted bureaucrats pave this island over. It broke my heart." Lester was thinking about his beloved light rail scheme. The legislature was talking about it again. Why hadn't they listened in the sixties? *It's too expensive.* Well, it was thirty times more expensive now. Cheap bastards.

"Men are stupid, no doubt about that," said his father, as if he could read Lester's thoughts. "That's what the afterlife is all about." He stood and stretched his arms. "Before anything happens you have to look at your mistakes in the mirror."

"So there's no heaven and hell," said Lester.

"Oh, sure, until you get tired of it. Then you move on. I don't think your mother is going to get tired of her hell anytime soon. She's covering it with plastic."

"I thought hell was hot," said Lester. "Doesn't the plastic melt?"

"Depends on your state of mind." His father sat down knee to knee with Lester and looked him in the eye. "A man goes to his rabbi and says, 'My wife is trying to poison me.' The rabbi says, 'Let me talk to her.' So he goes away and talks to the wife and comes back to the man, who says, 'What do you think?' The rabbi answers, 'My advice to you: take the poison.' Your mother's hell is ice cold."

That jibed with what Lester knew about his mother. She covered all her furniture with plastic. Mrs. Higata left her house to Lester's son Paul, and he never bothered to change anything. Every time a girl moved in with him, the first thing she tried to do was take the plastic off the furniture. Paul said he liked the plastic. It meant he didn't have to be careful about sitting on the couch when he was dirty. When Paul got married, the plastic finally went. His wife cut it off one day when he went fishing. The red and blue silk shimmered for a year, until Mikki had a baby. Now everything was covered in mashed bananas and Cheerios.

When his wife, Katherine, woke Lester to give him his medicine, he was laughing at a joke his father had been telling him about engineers and air conditioning in hell.

"That must have been some dream," she said, holding out two pills and a glass of water.

"My father was sitting here with me telling me lawyer jokes."

He couldn't tell a believer like Katherine that heaven and hell were just way stations until you decided you were ready to roam the timeless highways like a hobo.

"Was your mother there?" Katherine sat down beside him. She was wearing black slacks and a pink blouse. She'd been to see her masseuse that morning. It was the only thing that helped her arthritis.

"Would I be laughing?" Lester asked.

"No," Katherine said. "You would not." She reached over and smoothed his hair. "What would you like for lunch?"

He stretched his feet out in front of him. The sun melted some of the creakiness in his old legs. How could he sleep in a wobbly lawn chair and not in his own comfortable bed at night?

"How about some soup? I could thaw some of that yellow pepper soup you like so much and make a cheese sandwich. I have some avocado, too."

Lester nodded. "That sounds good." He smiled at his wife. Her hair was white, but in some ways she was prettier than she'd been when he'd first seen her fifty-three years before, a *haole* nurse in his ward at Tripler after the war. The wounds in his leg had been so painful, but not as bad as the pictures of the war he carried in his mind. He was glad Paul hadn't seen the things he'd seen. He and Katherine had been afraid Paul would be sent to Vietnam, but his draft number was so high they didn't have to worry.

"Linda called," Katherine said. "She's coming over after lunch. She thought you might like a game of Scrabble."

"I like it when I beat my Ph.D. daughter," Lester said, and an hour later it looked as if he would beat her again when, on his first turn, he put down TOURING, using all seven letters, for which he got an extra fifty points and then doubled that because he'd gone first. However, after a little deliberation, Linda put down TEXTBOOK, using all her letters, too. The X was on a double-letter square. Lester was ahead, 136 to 80, but Linda was still in the game.

"Wow," said Linda, "I really pulled that one out. It's not really fair to use all your letters on your first turn." Her thick hair was cut short, and she was wearing a blue and white striped shirt with long sleeves.

"When you're good, you're good," Lester said. They were at the dining room table, the yellow *Laelia* in a jade-green ceramic pot on the buffet, ruffling the air around it with the deep gold of its petals. He could hear Katherine puttering around in the kitchen. She was singing. What was it? Oh, "The Tennessee Waltz." It had been on the radio when Linda was a baby. Katherine would listen to Lester's jazz albums, but she preferred Frank Sinatra and Bing Crosby. Lester tried not to make a face, but sometimes he couldn't help himself. Sinatra was okay, but Bing Crosby couldn't swing his way out of a paper bag.

"You look good, Dad. Rested." Linda was sorting her seven letters on the little wooden bench, her eyes narrowed with a fierce concentration she'd had even as a little girl working on a science project or reading a book or helping him in the yard or even washing rice.

"I had a nap this morning on the lanai. I dreamed I saw your grandfather," Lester said. He had MANGO and TF. Of course, that could be TANGO, too, though the M was worth more points.

"What did he have to say?" Linda didn't look up from her letters.

"He said when you don't have a body, you can really move around. I think he said time was porous without a body."

"It sounds as if your dad has been experiencing some string theory," Linda said, frowning at her letters. She looked up at Lester. "Charles has been reading this long article in The New Yorker about new physics research. He keeps interrupting the novel I'm reading and saying things like 'Do you know why Einstein's theory of relativity and quantum mechanics cancel each other out?'"

"Why?" Lester asked. Her letters were terrible. He could always tell by the way she frowned and moved her pieces around, one square here and another one there.

"Daddy, how should I know? I'm a psychologist. I think he said that Einstein could explain the way the universe worked, and quantum mechanics explains how the nuclear world works, but the equations for one don't translate for the other. Einstein was working on a theory that explained it all when he died, but he didn't make it. I think black holes are the problem."

"They always are," said Lester, and put down MANGO, using

one of the O's in Linda's TEXTBOOK. Then he picked out four new letters. He got a Q and a U. Was that luck or what?

"Great word, Dad. I have nothing." She put down MANATEE.

"You saved my *okole* with that M. Charles said a black hole is so dense no light can escape from it."

"Like my mother," Lester said, but he didn't laugh. What if his mother showed up the way his father had?

"Pretty much. She was a class-A bitch. How did you and Auntie Gloria turn out so normal?"

"Gloria's normal?" Lester said. His sister was still playing golf and wearing short skirts even though she was seventy-six.

"She's not in jail, is she?" Linda looked up. Katherine had come into the dining room.

"I'm going to run to Kokua Market," she said to Lester. "Do you want anything?"

"Get some of that Ezekiel cereal, plain, not cinnamon," Lester said. "And some rice milk." They'd started eating organic after Lester's lung cancer was diagnosed.

"It looks as if it might rain later," Katherine said. "I'm going to go now, so I don't get caught in it." She kissed Lester and then Linda and walked out to the carport.

"And some Fujis," Lester called after her. She waved and he watched her pull out of the driveway and disappear down the street toward Makiki Heights Drive.

"What are you and Mommy going to do for New Year's Eve?" Linda asked.

"Nothing," said Lester. "Same as always. We can't stay up that late anymore."

"It's 2000, the millennium, Daddy. You have to stay up for this one. Charles and I are having a party. Why don't you and Mommy come?" When Linda smiled, she had lines around her eyes and mouth. She was forty-eight. His little girl was middle aged.

"We'll think about it," Lester said.

"That means no," said Linda. There was no gray in her dark hair, but that meant nothing. She probably had it colored. She shuffled her letters again.

"String theory says that the smallest examples of matter are strings rather than particles. The string vibrates like the string of a violin, so it changes in different circumstances. I love the idea of the universe being music. I just wish Einstein could have lived to see it happen. The atom bomb was not what he had in mind when he was thinking about the structure of the universe."

"Einstein believed in God," Lester said.

"Yeah," she nodded, "but I don't think it was quite the same one the Baptist church believes in. The principle is the same."

"I suppose the math is different."

"Very funny, but watch out. I have some good letters now, and I'm going to trounce you. You will be weeping."

Lester put down QUARK.

"Daddy," Linda said. "That's fabulous. It's enough to make you believe in God."

"Or mathematics," said Lester. He beat her 319 to 281.

After Linda left, Lester went through his albums until he found the LP he was looking for, Lester Young playing with Billie Holiday. Lester had a CD player, but he liked the sound of the records better, even with the pops and scratches. This wasn't his favorite Young record. He loved the one with the Oscar Peterson Trio, especially "There Will Never Be Another You," but he was in a Billie Holiday mood. He lay back on the living room couch and let the music flow around him like water. He was lucky Katherine had never wanted to cover their furniture with plastic.

Billie was singing "The Very Thought of You." Lester loved the line about "living in a daydream." Then, when she stopped singing Lester Young's sax came in, so relaxed and cool, moving around the melody, that sweet stutter, almost like a strut, and then the cascade of notes just before her voice came in again. The way she said the word *flower* was like an orchid blooming; she opened up the word with her voice, and Young's sax was a river that voice was sailing on, sometimes smooth, sometimes choppy, but always buoyant and moving along toward the deep sea.

Lester Young died when he was forty-nine. What had they done to him in the army? Lester was sure those years had killed him. He couldn't believe how they treated black people when he was in basic training in Mississippi. He'd seen a white bus driver push an old woman down the steps of the bus so Lester and his friends could get on first. They'd picked up the woman and insisted she board first, but she wouldn't. You could see she was scared of the driver, and she had to ride that bus everyday.

When Lester opened his eyes, Minoru Higata was sitting on the green velvet chair by the living room window. Outside it was raining, one of those driving tropical storms that made it seem as if the world were ending. He hoped Katherine wasn't out in it.

"You're back," he said to his father. "I'm really dying this time, aren't I? Why did you leave before?"

"I wanted you to see Linda one more time. She's a good girl. That Paul's a mess." Minoru Higata was wearing a tuxedo jacket this time, plaid shorts, and black rubber slippers. What was the afterlife like? Lester guessed he would be finding out any minute now, though he supposed "minutes" were a thing of the past.

"It's funny, everyone says Paul's just like you." Lester sat up and rubbed his face.

"That's because they don't know me. I would have ripped those plastic covers off your mother's furniture the first day. He's lucky he found a girl crazy enough to marry him." He crossed his legs, leaned back, and laced his fingers together at the base of his skull.

"I did enjoy our game," said Lester. "I love to beat her."

"Are you sure you beat her?" His father had that sly smile Lester remembered when he was saying something he knew would drive his wife crazy.

"She lets me win?" Lester felt time falling away like water does when you're coming up out of the waves at the beach.

"She's a good little actress," said his father. He stood up and held his hand out to Lester.

"Well, she fooled me," Lester said. The record was finished, the needle moving in the final band, over and over. He stood up and put his hand in his father's. He could have been eight instead of almost eighty.

"No fool like an old fool," said his father, opening the front door.

The rain was really coming down now, like a wall between one room and another. Lester loved a good rain. It cleared the air and made the earth smell sweet and new again. He was going to miss Honolulu. Sure there were too many cars, and the kids were acting so crazy with ice and all those other drugs, but still it was paradise. People talked about the island as if it were ruined. It was different. A lot of the old places were gone. The Aloha Tower was so *manini* now in the cluster of tall buildings downtown. Wo Fat's had closed, but the market in Chinatown was still busy as an anthill, mangoes and bananas piled high and long radishes like the arms of some sea creature.

He followed his father through the door, and as he walked into the rain, the house disappeared along with the roads and all the buildings. He was moving through the jungle that had covered O'ahu before it had that name, when wild boar roamed the underbrush, and red and yellow plumed birds glided in the treetops. Was he a particle or a string? He felt the music of the universe vibrating in him, the rain washing over him, washing the years away, the roads, the skyscrapers, all the strip clubs by Ala Moana, H3 to Kāne'ohe that desecrated the sacred Hawaiian lands, the military bases, and the sad karaoke bars near Schofield Barracks. It was all gone, and he moved through the green land with its fishing pools, *heiau*, and taro fields, the world opening up, timeless and relaxed as a saxophone solo by a broken man, whose voice was too sweet for this world.

Iniki
Chicken
1992

After Iniki the island of Kaua'i looked like the photos of Europe my father took right after World War II, but instead of armies, winds over 150 miles an hour had leveled houses, restaurants, shopping centers, hotels, even cinder block schools and government buildings. All the trees on the lush Hanalei coast were stripped bare—as if winter, so long a stranger to the Hawaiian Islands, had decided to pay a surprise visit and left in its wake a January landscape of bare branches haunted by isolated mynah birds. Jerry, a carpenter I'd worked with on a high-rise in Honolulu, said it was like Vietnam, napalm without the fire. Bands of construction workers were camping on the beach, so Opera Bob and I were lucky we ran into Jerry at the airport.

"Paul," Jerry yelled and thumped me on the back. "Welcome to Hiroshima."

He took us to a house where twenty or so men were living, men who were there to rebuild Kaua'i, some no better than thieves, there to take what they could from the shattered island. Others, like Opera Bob and Jerry, were real craftsmen, who couldn't resist the lure of insurance money, but a few, like me, were running away from something so bad that rebuilding Kaua'i was a child's game, a simple matter of taking pieces of wood and nailing them together.

That first night the house was a scene from the Wild West. By the light of a kerosene lamp, seven or eight guys were sitting around a table drinking shots of whiskey and playing poker. When we walked in, they turned and stared at us, two skinny guys with backpacks. None of them had shaved in a month, and they were smoking hand-rolled cigarettes and *pakalolo*. I thought the six-shooters were going to start blazing any minute, and all I was carrying was my toolbox and a Skilsaw. Finally, they laughed and went back to their game. Jerry showed us where we could stow our tools and bags. Headphones clamped on, Bob crawled into his sleeping bag listening to Mozart, but in five minutes I could hear soft rhythmic snores like the purring of a cat over the muffled sound of the orchestra.

I couldn't sleep thinking about Lani. What would she do when she found out I'd left Honolulu? Call and let the phone ring twenty or thirty times? Leave hysterical messages? Call my sister and beg her to tell her where I was? Good old Linda, she could keep her mouth shut. I was such a sap. Lani would find another guy. Oh, wait, I forgot. She already had another guy, plus her husband, and she was trying to lasso me in again to fill her spare moments. I went to sleep in the middle of a revenge fantasy of calling her husband and her boyfriend and playing the frantic tapes she'd made on my answering machine. "Paul, I know you're there. Pick up. Pick up. I'm dying without you. I can't live without your body."

Can you believe it, the mother of two?

The next day Jerry introduced us to Mr. and Mrs. Imamoto, whose house near Hanalei was blown away in the storm. They were living with her sister's family, seven people in one little house: Mr. and Mrs. Imamoto, the sister Rosalie and her husband, Derek Kuono, as well as the Kuonos' grown daughter, Natalie, her husband, and their four-year-old son.

"It's crazy," Mrs. Imamoto said to us. "We got to get out of there before Natalie's husband blows. He's making these funny sounds all the time."

"What kind of sounds?" asked Bob, his Adam's apple rising and falling like a barometer before a storm.

"Animal noises," said Mrs. Imamoto. "Like pigs or cats. How can you eat dinner with someone across the table going meow, meow, oink, oink? It's worse when he starts barking. Sometimes I wake up in the middle of the night and think someone's beating a dog, but it's Larry standing outside barking at the dog next door." She shook her head, which was covered like a helmet with thick gray hair. She was in her mid-sixties, but trim and energetic, like one of those spruce short-haired terriers who dances around, its nose into everything. Mr. Imamoto was retired from the city. He said exactly two sentences the whole time we worked for him, but he toiled beside us like a slave to rebuild his house. Maybe Larry's barking was giving him the willies, too.

The Imamotos showed us a photo of what their house had looked like before Iniki. The only thing they'd saved was a book of photographs and a teriyaki grill. Like a lot of houses in the islands, it was built off the ground and had Japanese elements, especially in the lines of the roof. Bob and I showed them photos of houses we'd built, which seemed to make them happy, that and the fact I was part Japanese.

"Your name is Higata, so your mother must be *haole*," said Mrs. Imamoto. We were standing in what used to be her front yard, staring at the shards of broken lumber and damp household debris, crushed porcelain, twisted furniture, shattered windows.

I nodded, estimating how long it would take us to clear the lot of fallen trees and the little that was left of the Imamotos' house.

"Where's your mother from?" Mrs. Imamoto asked, shielding her eyes from the sun.

"Ohio." I figured a couple of days to clear the yard. Getting materials was another story. Jerry said the lumber guys were starting to gouge people.

"Oh, my other sister lives in Dayton. Her husband works for GM. He's a *haole*, too."

"There are a lot of *haoles* in Ohio," I said.

She laughed and punched me in the arm. "I like you," she said. "Your skinny friend, too."

"When Captain Cook's ships anchored in Kaua'i, 13,000 people were living on the Nā Pali coast." Derek Kuono was grilling chicken on the Imamotos' hibachi. Mr. Imamoto was silently tending another grill with yams and potatoes wrapped in tin foil for Opera Bob and the Kuono's daughter Natalie, both vegetarians. Mrs. Imamoto and her sister were inside the house making sushi and salad. I'd seen no sign of Barking Larry and his family. Derek Kuono's house was the only one on the street that had not been flattened by Iniki's winds. All around him was devastation, but he hadn't lost a tree.

"They grew taro, coconuts. Now some wild guys hike back into the mountains and grow the *pakalolo*. They even use the terraces of the old Hawaiians and their irrigation system." He turned the chicken thighs with a long fork and brushed them with shoyu. He was a big man with a softly rounded torso.

"No one lives there now, because the girls were too friendly with the sailors. Syphilis and smallpox. By the time the missionaries got here and explained how they should keep only unto each other, it was too late. Those sailors nearly destroyed our whole culture."

The darkening sky was shot through with red and gold like one of the kimonos my Japanese grandmother had hung on the walls of her living room. A young couple was walking down the street toward us, a little boy in a Batman cape racing ahead of them on a tricycle. The woman was about six inches taller than the man, towering over him like a Gauguin goddess who had gotten hold of Carmen Mirandas costume trunk. Her chest was framed by a white off-the-shoulder blouse and her ripe bottom barely contained in a pair of banana-yellow capri pants. She looked like a younger feminine version of Derek Kuono. Her companion, I supposed, was Barking Larry, a little Filipino with lank hair and an expression on his face that seemed to be sucking the light out of the air around him.

"Captain Cook wasn't such a bad guy," Derek said, waving at his daughter and her husband. "He saw what the *haole* diseases did in Tahiti, so he gave strict orders to his men with syphilis to stay away from the local women. If they didn't, then flogging. But what was one *haole* man against sex and disease?"

After work, I'd meet Jerry at Pammy-Tam's, a local bar that had managed to reopen. Even Opera Bob was not unknown to drink a beer from time to time, seeing as how no animal suffered to create it, though he was not much of a wine drinker, and I never saw him touch hard liquor. However, this was a time in my life when gin and its darker cousins became if not my best friends then very intimate acquaintances, ones I could go to in the middle of the night, and they would sweet talk me through the hours from two to five when I ran the movies of Lani over in my mind, remembering every kiss, drink, fight, and lie, especially the lies, biting and tearing at me like hungry sharks.

At Pammy-Tam's we met Isaac Miyasaki, a tall guy with a pockmarked face, who was living in one of the few hotels that hadn't been flattened by Iniki's winds. He was an insurance adjuster from Honolulu.

"American Home Guaranty," he said, raising the considerable weight of one of Pammy-Tam's mai tais.

"Have saw, will travel," said Jerry. We slid onto the bar stools around Isaac and ordered.

"I should just write the checks out to you," Isaac said. "Faster that way." He was lining up his empty glasses in front of him.

"How'd you become an insurance agent?" I asked Isaac after we'd discussed the current state of chaos on Kaua'i. The bartender placed a sweating ten-ounce glass in front of me, the honey-colored liquid swimming over the sparkling ice.

"A direct calling from God," said Isaac.

"I didn't know God called insurance agents," said Opera Bob, knocking back his beer. "I thought it was only ministers and priests and guys like that."

Isaac turned to Bob and looked at him as though he could see through him to the other side. "I can see theology is not your strong suit. Am I right?"

Bob shrugged. "I guess so. I'm more interested in music."

"A fine calling," slurred Isaac, "but if you were a theologian you would know that God calls everyone to his role in life. Some call it destiny, some call it . . ." He paused, an index finger raised as if searching for a word.

"Karma," I said.

He turned to me, "Thank you. 'Karma,' but God has set the pieces in motion."

"Sounds like Calvin," I said, taking the first swallow of my mai tai, the rum sluicing my throat like rain on a dusty road going nowhere.

"Ah," Isaac said, "a fellow theologian," and raised his glass to toast me. "Yes, God had a plan for me. Some might call it a trap, but I call it a plan in the form of Rosalind Yee. God works in mysterious ways, and he knew the way to lure me into my rightful role as an insurance adjuster was through Rosalind Yee's cupcake breasts."

"God's used that plan for a lot of guys," said Jerry.

"A good plan is above rubies," said Isaac draining his glass and placing it in a line with three other empty glasses. "Wendell," he said to the bartender. "You make an excellent mai tai, my man."

Wendell pushed his thick black-framed glasses up the bridge of his nose and smiled. Wendell was Pammy-Tam's son. He was a student at UH but had come back to Kaua'i after Iniki to help his mom.

"Uh-oh," whispered Isaac, looking at the door. "It's Mr. Chicken."

A skinny *haole* guy stepped into Pammy-Tam's and surveyed the room. His hair hadn't been cut in a while. He looked like one of Rasputin's acolytes.

A girl waved, her pale arm fluorescent in the dim room. "Donny, over here," she called, and he went to join her and a group of people who had a table on the lanai where tiny white lights sparkled like stars in the branches of an old banyan tree.

"Why do you call him Mr. Chicken?" asked Opera Bob, but Isaac had begun the complicated task of extricating himself from the barstool.

"God has a plan for all of you," he called to the room as he left, stumbling over chairs and bumping into Pammy-Tam herself before he made it through the door. She shook her head and continued to wipe tables with a dirty rag.

Jerry pointed to the wild-haired Rasputin. "That's the guy I was telling you about. He's a great framer. He's finishing up a house near Po'ipū. His girlfriend lives in Hanalei. I bet you could get him to work on your house."

I nodded and walked over and introduced myself. Within five minutes, I had Donny lined up to work on the Imamotos' house as soon as we picked up the lumber.

I met Mikki at the Safeway in Līhu'e. I noticed her because she was pushing two carts of kids cereal: Captain Crunch, Count Chocula, Fruit Loops, Trix. How many kids could a woman that slim have? Then I thought of Lani, skin and bones and the mother of two huge children.

I saw Mikki again in the parking lot. She was struggling to push two carts of bagged groceries, so I just started pushing one. When she saw I didn't look like an ax murderer, she led the way to her van.

I asked her out to dinner the next night, and she said yes. We agreed to meet at Pammy-Tam's. I don't know why I asked her to go out with me, since she wasn't my type. She was short with a muscular body and lightly freckled skin. Her long dark-red hair was braided and lay on her back like an exotic snake, the sun glinting off its scales, red and gold.

Just before I left O'ahu my sister Linda showed me a photograph of my mother as a young woman, boyishly slim with big blue eyes and dark curly hair. "Does she remind you of anyone you know?" Linda asked.

"Yeah," I said, "Lani."

"No, every woman you've ever gone out with," she said. "If you put them all together it would be like a police lineup. If a short blonde with big breasts smiles at you, smile back. Ask her out for a drink. Talk to her. You don't have to get married. Try a Japanese girl. It wouldn't kill you."

Linda would have been proud of me asking Mikki out. She was flat chested, but she had red hair and a waist and hips.

Derek Kuono's *tutu* had taught him how to speak Hawaiian.

"It's different on Kaua'i," he said. "Līhu'e not Honolulu. There's not so much pressure to act *haole*. My *tutu* remembered when Lili'oukalani was queen. She thought having a queen was the way to go. She'd always talk about Queen Elizabeth, Queen Victoria, Indira Gandhi, Golda Meir. She'd say a woman always runs a country better than a man because she's never got to prove her dick is bigger than the other guys'."

"She taught me all the words and how the *'aumākua*, the family gods, protect you. That's why my house never fell down in Iniki. It was protected by my *'aumākua*. I tell my wife, 'In Hawai'i the Hawaiian gods work. Your Buddha and Jesus are never going to do nothing here.'"

He and I were clearing the remnants of the Imamotos' house, piling the rubbish near the road. Opera Bob and Mr. Imamoto had taken the truck into Līhu'e to pick up lumber.

"You know," he said, swinging an axe in an arc over his broad back and bringing it down on a palm trunk that was tangled in the debris of door frames and flooring, "the old Hawaiians really studied the weather." The palm trunk fell into two pieces. Derek picked up one end, I took the other and we lugged it to the street.

"They have all kinds of words to describe the rain. *Lelehuna* is a light rain blown by the wind, and *uakea* is mist like the spray from the top of a wave. Iniki was *kūpiki'ō*. That means raging like a crazy person. It was like that in Iniki, like the voice of God saying 'Get ready, you're *pau*.'"

Mikki said, "It could take a long time for things to get back to normal."

We were at Pammy-Tam's. Isaac was at the bar talking to Mr. Chicken and his girlfriend. Mikki worked for the Ohana Project. She went around and helped people do ordinary things like fill out forms, pay electric bills, shop for groceries. *'Ohana* is the Hawaiian word for family, but it also means acting like family.

"You know, at first, everyone is out of their minds with happiness because they aren't dead, and that can last for a couple of months. You're trying to figure stuff out. You think, Hey, I can lick this."

Mikki had unbraided her hair, and it shimmered around her earnest face like a russet halo, a sun setting in a forest against her dark green dress.

"But it's not that easy. One day the Red Cross leaves. You want to leave, too, and not stand in lines and deal with all the red tape of rebuilding your house and dealing with all the asshole insurance people and carpenters." She grinned at me. "Maybe you have to have two jobs to get what you need for your family. Maybe you think, It's not really worth it, all this work, and for what? Another hurricane could just come out of the ocean and take it away again. Maybe you start drinking too much or beating up on your wife and kids. It takes a long time to get over something like Iniki. A couple of years, maybe. Funny thing is, it can make you stronger. People take better care of their neighbors. They know their neighbors. Something like Iniki makes the government get its act together. People can't say, *It can never happen to us.* It did happen, so what are we going to do if it happens again?"

I told her about Barking Larry, who was now living in a tent in the backyard. Mrs. Imamoto said it was to be closer to his best friend Polo, the German shepherd next door. Everyone was relieved he was out of the house, but sometimes Roy, his little boy, would sleep out in the tent with him. That usually kept Larry from barking, but sometimes it didn't, and the noise scared the little boy. "Some people never recover," Mikki said. "The winds take more than their houses."

Bob saw Lani when he went into Līhu'e to buy some CDs. He'd just discovered Baroque opera and wanted to get a copy of anything with a counter-tenor singing the castrato's role.

"Can you believe that they used to cut off a guy's balls so he could sing like a woman?" Bob said. He'd just finished sawing a four-by-four for the frame of the Imamotos' house.

"Absolutely," said Donny, alias Mr. Chicken, pushing back a thatch of brown hair. It was his first day on the job. "In Chile and Argentina they did stuff like that to students because they didn't like being ruled by the military, and then they killed them. For the singers it was a career decision. I'd say it was a step up in the evolutionary chain."

"You'll never guess who I saw in Līhu'e," Bob said. He was inserting *L'incoronazione di Poppea* in the boom box.

My heart was pounding like the Tahitian drummers I saw on an eighth-grade field trip to the Polynesian Cultural Center, but I continued hammering threepenny nails into the beam between the living room and the kitchen.

"That crazy married girlfriend of yours came up behind me at the saimin stand near the lumber yard."

I couldn't look at him. "What did she say?"

"What do you think? 'Where's Paul?'"

I sat down on a stack of lumber near the frame of the dining room door.

"Don't worry. I told her we were working near Po'ipū."

"She didn't follow you?"

"Is she that weird?"

"She came to Kaua'i, left her husband and kids to track me down. That's not weird?"

"She had one of her kids with her."

"You're kidding. Which one?"

"How should I know? All kids look alike to me."

"One's a girl and one's a boy."

"Oh," Bob said, "she had the girl with her. Did you want me to tell her where you were?"

I groaned like someone who had just been harpooned. For the rest of the day I looked over my shoulder, dreading the sound of

Lani's ragged muffler on the dirt road leading to the Imamotos' house. It wasn't until late in the afternoon when we were cleaning up that I realized she wouldn't have brought her car to Kaua'i. She could be driving in any car down any road. That night as I lay awake in my sleeping bag, I prayed, if not to God, then to the universe, "Make me invisible. Hide me from the sight of that crazy woman. Make me into a piece of the sky. Let me fold myself into the earth." I knew I couldn't be trusted not to start it all over again, walk into her web of lies as if she were the woman I thought she was the first time I kissed her.

Donny, Opera Bob, and I had worked on the Imamotos' house for a couple of days before Bob thought to ask, "Why does Isaac call you Mr. Chicken?"

Donny paused and looked at the sky. He was nut brown, dark as a local. He said his dad was part Cherokee. He'd lived on O'ahu since he was eight years old.

"I have this thing about eating chicken."

Bob tensed. He got excited when he sniffed out anyone with eating obsessions. It was the only thing besides music and carpentry he was interested in. "You don't eat meat?"

"Oh, I eat meat," said Donny, "I just don't eat chicken."

"Why chicken?" said Bob.

Donny drew himself up like a preacher starting on a two-hour rant. "I was a chicken-eater like anyone else until I came here after Iniki. The storm destroyed houses, hotels, everything, so it stood to reason that chicken coops would be *pau*, too. There were chickens running wild everywhere, pecking at the dirt on the side of roads, in deserted parking lots, on the beach. I pulled into the lot of a little store near Waimea and saw a couple of chickens eating cigarette butts. Right then I swore I'd never eat chicken again.

"The more I thought about it, the more I realized how right I was. Birds are nervous creatures. Look at the sky; they're always flying. Look at the ground—always pecking. In China they kill a rhinoceros, grind up his horns, and use the dust for an aphrodisiac. You eat a steak, pound your chest and say, Strong like bull. You eat a chicken, and what are you? Nervous. My grandmother loved chicken. She ate it all her life—fried chicken, roasted chicken, and at the end Chicken McNuggets. How did she end up? Eight years in a nursing home, not even knowing her own name, my aunt stealing all the money the old lady had saved so she wouldn't end up in a place like that. I bet Ronald Reagan loved chicken, too. I'm not saying it's a conspiracy, trying to kill us through chickens, but look at the facts. Thirty years ago girls started their periods when they were thirteen or fourteen. Now it's nine and ten. Why? Because of the estrogen they pump into chickens to make their breasts plumper. It's going to start happening to men soon—low sperm count. I'll be considered a prophet. One day I opened my car door and saw a neat little pyramid of chicken bones. I took it as a sign."

I couldn't help myself. "What kind of sign?" I asked.

"A sign from God," Donny said.

"God was telling you to stop eating chicken? With a whole universe on his hands, he sure is interested in the little things."

"You know what they say." Donny pulled a four-by-four up and nailed it in place. "God's in the details."

Maybe that was the reason the world is such a mess. God was paying too much attention to *manini* things like the dietary habits of construction workers and letting the big issues slide. But I was feeling benevolent toward God, because Lani had not shown up. I called my sister in Honolulu, and she said she'd seen Lani the day before when she went to check on my house. Lani had been parked across the street in her beatup brown Chevy.

"Did you talk to her?"

"I said, 'Hi.' She looked terrible. Her hair was orange and she was skin and bones. She asked where you were, and I said I didn't know, and she said I wouldn't tell her even if I knew, and I told her she was right, and she drove away."

This conversation fed my insomnia for a couple of nights. The whole scene between Linda and Lani was as clear as if I had been there filming a documentary. Little Mrs. Niitani next door was outside watering her banana trees while Linda stood on the street talking to Lani who sat in her ugly brown car. The sky was paint blue, and I could hear the dull roar of traffic from the highway. My only comfort was that Lani wasn't roaming Kaua'i, waiting to pounce on me like a hungry dog.

The day we finished framing the Imamotos' house, Natalie Kuono ran up to the job site crying. "Where's my daddy?" she called, looking around the site. "Uncle Hiro," she sobbed to Mr. Imamoto, "where's Daddy?"

"He's not here," I said, afraid that she might collapse before getting an answer out of Mr. Imamoto.

She turned to me. "We've got to do something. I can't take it anymore." She was wearing red cotton shorts and a white eyelet halter top that exposed the soft brown of her stomach.

Mr. Imamoto put his arm around her.

"He's got Roy barking now," Natalie said. "My little boy is barking like a dog."

"My girlfriend works for the Ohana Project," I said. It felt funny to call Mikki my girlfriend. I hadn't used the word for a long time. Lani was married, so I couldn't use it for her.

Natalie was sitting on the ground. The soft flesh of her abdomen rolled over the top of her red shorts like a loaf of brown bread.

"Maybe Mikki could send someone over to talk to Larry," I said.

She looked up, "Yeah? You think they have somebody who can speak dog language? You think they have somebody who can go to the backyard and bark some sense into him?"

"Come on, girlie." Mr. Imamoto helped her get up and led her down the street. She towered over him like a young healthy tree, the sun glimmering in her thick curly hair.

"I blame it on chickens," said Donny from his perch in the rafters.

I watched Natalie and Mr. Imamoto walk away and wished I had something as ordinary as chickens to blame for my sleepless nights.

I was in Līhu'e picking up a couple of bottles of rum for the long nights in Hanalei when Lani finally tracked me down.

"Paul," she said. The sound of her voice rushed through my

veins like battery acid. She was wearing a pair of faded jeans and a shirt that had once been white. Even though she was *hapa-haole*, she was pale, her skin like parchment. She looked as if she hadn't eaten in weeks, her skinny arms accentuating her hands, big and bony as a man's.

I should have left right then, but I couldn't. I remembered her husband telling me about the time the police found her in Hilo dancing on a park bench with only her bathing suit top on. The whole family was crazy. Her brother Chris preached on a corner in Waikīkī, ranting about the end of the world. If only the world would end, I thought as I looked at her ragged nails and the dark crescent moon of black metal between her gums and capped front teeth. Who had really knocked out her teeth? She'd told me half a dozen different stories.

"Paul." She said it like a ghost, with the disembodied whisper of the spirit world Derek Kuono had told me about, a world that existed alongside our own, just as real but not made of flesh and blood. "Why did you leave me?"

I turned and walked out of the store. The parking lot was nearly empty.

"Why?" she screamed, following me.

"Lani, what are you doing here?" I said, the fierce whisper echoing in my skull like a bell. "You know why I left."

She caught up with me and grabbed my wrist and fell on her knees. "Please fuck me. I can't live without it. Just fuck me and I'll go away." And she would, too, leaving me like a sailor leaves a prostitute. It had happened too many times before.

I ripped my wrist away from her hands, but she grabbed at my ankles. A few people had gathered in a small knot by the door of the market.

"Lani." I was still whispering. Her head jerked up and she followed my gaze to the little group of people: a couple of old men in chinos and a woman and her little boy. She turned to them. "All I want is a little sex," she yelled, "but he won't give it to me. What kind of man is that?" The woman hustled her little boy into the store.

"You want me to call the police?" one of the old men said to me.

"Do you want him to?" I asked her.

She was back on her knees like a tattered nun. "No, Paul. You know what I want."

"Call them," I said to the old man, who turned and went into the store.

"Bastard," she screamed. I don't know if she meant me or the old man or maybe her big *haole* father, who had chased her and her brother down Lipona Street with a belt, screaming. He was still chasing her though he'd been dead for years, but there was nothing I could do. I'd tried, but she'd squeezed my heart so dry I didn't think I had one any more, just the remnants, parched rust-colored fragments like old metal in a junkyard.

When the police came, she was rocking back and forth in a little ball on the pavement, her bony arms wrapped around her knees. Her eyes were closed and she was moaning like a wounded animal.

I gave the police her husband's name and phone number. She didn't speak as they led her away. The foul-mouthed viper was gone, and in her place was a wounded little girl. This was the Lani who could make me do anything. The last I saw of her was the sad crook of her head in the back of that police cruiser.

I called Mikki and she sent a Filipino guy she worked with over to see Larry. He drove up in an old Valiant. Derek, Natalie, and I were sitting in the front yard drinking rum and Cokes and cooking hamburgers on the grill. We pointed Mikki's friend in the direction of the backyard.

"You can't kill those cars," said Derek Kuono, looking at the Valiant.

Natalie started pacing, talking nonstop to her father and me. "You know, there was a hurricane in the Philippines when he was a little boy, and afterwards there was no food. Do you think that has something to do with his barking?"

I looked at Derek Kuono, but he just sat in his lawn chair like a brown god. He handed Natalie a fresh drink, which she swigged like a shipwrecked sailor.

"I like your outfit," he said to his daughter. She was wearing a red Chinese shirt and gold lamé leggings.

"Daddy, this is serious. What am I going to do?"

"Maybe this guy can help," he said, but she kept pacing and drinking, as if walking back and forth in straight lines was going to straighten out her life.

After about ten minutes, Mikki's friend and Larry walked into the front yard.

"Larry's going to come with me for a few days," he said.

"Why," Natalie croaked as if she had a gecko stuck in her throat.

"I need help," Larry said, his voice like a shivering mouse. "Let me go," he said to his wife. "I'll be back soon."

Natalie kissed the top of his head and watched him drive away in the old Valiant. "What if he doesn't come back?" she asked the road on which her husband was disappearing.

"He'll be back," said Derek Kuono, and when he spoke it was as if the spirit of the place had spoken, the 'aumakua protecting his little piece of land from the wild storms of the world.

By the time I left Kaua'i, I had nearly forgotten about Lani. The scar was still there, but it was faded white on my dark skin. Mikki wanted me to stay, but I missed Honolulu, missed the house my Japanese grandmother had left me, even missed old Mrs. Niitani next door always begging me to fix a window or gutter.

One day just before I left, we were at the beach. Mikki was wearing a long-sleeved shirt and a hat to protect her skin from the sun. It was one of those days that only come in dreams, the sky so blue it seems transparent.

A man was walking up the beach with his wife and two daughters. The younger girl was about nine years old, and she was whining. Suddenly the man exploded and kicked the little girl. The mother and older girl froze, as did everyone on the beach. Time seemed to stop in the few seconds between the kick and the moment the girl began wailing. The mother pulled her arm. "Shut up," she said. "Shut up," while the man stalked up the beach.

Mikki ran up to the woman and said, "I can help you. Let me help you."

"Mind your own business," the woman snarled.

"He kicked her," Mikki said, reaching out for the little girl, who jumped away from her.

"Don't make it worse," the woman said. "Leave us alone," and she dragged the crying girl toward the road where her husband waited in the car. The older girl followed, head down, hair covering her face.

Mikki ran after them, and I ran after her. What might the man do to a stranger if he could kick his own daughter? The woman and the girls piled into the car.

"I have your license number," Mikki shouted at the car as it sped away.

"What kind of man kicks a child?" she asked me, but all I could think of was Larry barking at the dog next door and Lani moaning in the liquor store parking lot. The girl's wailing had been feral, like an animal with its leg in a trap. What stories were they recounting too terrible for human words?

When we finished the Imamotos' house, they had a big party to celebrate and to thank us for doing such a good job. Bob had gotten carried away with the curling red gables and gold trim, as if creating a set for *Madame Butterfly* rather than Mrs. Imamoto's brand of Buddhist Christianity. Mr. Imamoto had strung Christmas lights around the perimeter of his little yard, and he and Derek Kuono had dug a pit and were roasting a pig. There was a table out front loaded with food that people in the neighborhood had brought: fried chicken, lasagna, potato salad, macaroni salad, sushi, kim chee, watermelon from Moloka'i. Bob had hooked up a sound system and was playing the overture from *The Marriage of Figaro*, which the tradewinds carried over the budding trees and up toward the clouds.

"Before Iniki," said Mrs. Imamoto, "we never knew most of these people. Now look: we know everybody. And I have a new house, much better than the old one."

"A good house," said Mr. Imamoto. Bob and I looked at each other. Had he spoken?

Larry was back and he'd stopped barking. He had his arm around Natalie, who was wearing a magenta *holokū*, a form-fitting local dress that skimmed the grass and made her look like a goddess next to the other women in their shorts and muumuus.

When the pig was done, Derek Kuono and Mr. Imamoto dug it out of the *imu* and peeled off the burlap and banana leaves and carried it on its little platform of wire mesh to the already groaning table. Mrs. Imamoto asked the pastor of her church to say grace. While the succulent aromas of roasted pork wafted in the air along with Mozart, a *haole* man with a crewcut said, "Dear God in Heaven, bless this food to the nourishment of our bodies. Bless this family in its new beginning as you blessed the world with the resurrection of your son Jesus Christ. In His name we pray, Amen."

A little chorus of amens echoed in the crowd. Natalie and Larry's little boy said, "Amen, dig in." Everyone laughed and piled the food on their plates.

Looking at all the people gathered around the table, I wondered how so many different faces could be made in the image of one God? Maybe the Hawaiians were right, and there were many gods: Pele, who ruled from her molten palace in the heart of the volcano; Laka, who moved in the swaying hips and savage beat of the hula; Kāne, father of all living beings, the sun, water, and trees; Kū, the ferocious god of war; Kanaloa, who ruled the spirit world, the dwelling place of all those who had given up the cloak of flesh.

But if there was only one God what could he possibly be like? Was he Derek Kuono's dark spirit who whipped up the oceans to give voice to his anger or was he Isaac Miyasaki's fussy bureaucrat, sending teenaged girls out with their pert breasts to lure men into their allotted places in life? Or was he the great Buddha mind of my father's ancestors? What kind of being might be in charge of a world where men barked like dogs, kicked their own children, thought chickens caused you to lose your mind? He was a funny god, a god Groucho Marx might have imagined, one who liked a good laugh at the expense of His creation. Sometimes such a world was too much to take, and the only recourse seemed to be howling like a dog or something as ordinary as *'ohana*. Call it family, call it love—it's the thing that brings us together and rips us apart like a storm coming from the vast stretch of the ocean. We wake up one morning with the wind racing toward us like an animal, and nothing is ever the same.

Mr.
Manago's
Mango
Trees
1988

Fujio Manago always knew his son Roland had a keen eye for business. Mr. Manago said Roland would go far, and he did get as far away from Hawai'i as the west coast of the mainland, going to USC while that lazy Winston Nakamura next door barely finished high school. Mr. Manago and old Mrs. Nakamura talked about their boys over the fence that separated their backyards. Helen Nakamura was a little woman, spare and sinewy as the branches of the plumeria trees that shaded the front of her house. She raised her grandson Winston after her son, Teddy, and his wife were killed when their brakes failed going over the Pali in 1962. Their car broke through the barrier, careened across the other lane of traffic, empty at three in the morning, and flew over the side of the mountain like a mechanized bird toward the dark void of the Pacific Ocean. Everybody said Teddy was drunk, and they were probably right. Mr. Manago often wondered about Teddy Nakamura's last thoughts. Like Winston, Teddy had been a loser, but somehow he'd talked Debby Uyehara into marrying him, a girl so beautiful a room seemed to light up with her radiance. She reminded Mr. Manago of those paintings of Christian saints, a slight glow about her body. That was a long time ago. Debby Uyehara had been dead twenty-six years. Twenty-six years. How old did that make him? Seventy-eight. Who would have guessed he would live so long?

His wife died ten years after Teddy and Debby Uyehara. Cancer took her, the disease sucking the life out of her like a spider siphons the fluids from an insect in its web. Helen Nakamura held on for another ten years. She was almost ninety when she died, falling asleep one night in July to the sound of the traffic on Beretania and H1 and not waking the next morning. Winston found her when he brought her a cup of tea. This was a big surprise for Mr. Manago, Winston nursing his grandmother like a baby, moving back into the house when she couldn't shop for herself or lift the heavy sacks of rice to make her evening meal. Winston was a rough boy, but he did what his *obāsan* said. Even now, five years after her death, he tended her papaya trees as if she had gone to visit her cousins on the Big Island and would be back in a few days.

Trees were the key to Helen Nakamura's friendship with Fujio Manago. They met and talked as they tended their trees. Between their two houses, Mr. Manago owned an empty lot in which he planted six mango trees. Nothing could describe the pleasure he felt watching them grow, first as saplings and then as full trees, their limbs heavy every summer with green and then mauve-skinned fruit. Right in the middle of the city, he could smell the rich earth and pretend he was in Wai'anae, still a boy on his father's dairy farm, tending the cows and planting the vegetables they sold at the market in Chinatown. For years he had driven his truck down Farrington Highway to the farm, which was left to his older brother, and picked up loads of manure from the dairy barn to dress the soil around the roots of his mango trees. This was the secret of his mangoes' sweetness. They could break your heart with their sugary flesh: not the bright yellow of the sun in the noonday sky but the burnished orange glow as it fell into the Pacific, a caramelized, drugged light. He always brought Helen Nakamura some manure for her garden, for besides the stand of twenty papaya trees in her backyard she grew torch and shell ginger, bird of paradise, stephanotis, plumeria, and jasmine. The ginger in bloom was almost too much to bear, the red and pink blossoms filling the street with their wild scent. Winston must have watched his *obāsan* over the years or inherited her green thumb, because the garden looked exactly as it had when the old lady was alive, a little patch of old Hawai'i in the middle of Honolulu with its asphalt and concrete, the neon signs of drive-ins and stores that never seemed to stop flashing and the constant roar of H1, the highway that cut through the middle of Honolulu, one block from Lipona Street.

Mr. Manago sat in a plastic lawn chair under the spreading branches of his mango trees. Because he never sprayed his fruit, he sold most of the mangoes to the big health food store on King Street. Cow manure was the key. If the soil was strong, the plants would be strong and could fight insects on their own. The afternoon sun sent its pale light through the throng of branches and leaves, dancing in the trade winds off the ocean. Mr. Manago could watch this play of light and shadow on the ground for hours or close his eyes and feast on the scent of bitter earth and the sweetness of the plumerias blooming in Helen Nakamura's front yard. In 1963, she'd planted a cherry red variety, and now it was almost as tall as her house.

He closed his eyes and fell into a dream of Winston Nakamura playing dodge ball in the street in front of his house. Mr. Manago was on the other team with his son Roland. Winston threw the ball at him so hard, Mr. Manago woke up rubbing his arm, but it wasn't the ball that had awakened him but the rumble of Winston Nakamura's truck pulling up in front of the house next door. Winston waved at Mr. Manago and walked over and stood by the trunk of one of the mango trees.

"The mangoes *pau* for this year, yeah?" said Winston.

Mr. Manago nodded. "Best crop I ever had. Nine hundred and twenty-six."

"No way!" Winston shook his shaggy thatch of hair. It was stiff with sawdust and plaster. "You want one beer?" he asked, and

Mr. Manago saw he was carrying a six-pack, the cold beading up in the heat of the afternoon.

"Sure," he said, and Winston peeled a can from its plastic carrier and handed it to him.

"Pull up a chair," Mr. Manago said and nodded toward the stack of woven plastic lawn chairs leaning against his house. At his age, it was too much trouble to stand up anymore unless he had to. Winston brought a chair over and unfolded it in the shade of the mango trees. They sat in silence drinking their beers. Mr. Manago felt the iciness of the beer create a circle in the afternoon, completing the arc of the dappled light on the ground, the shadowy play of memory, and the scene unfolding in front of him.

"Where are you working now?" he asked Winston.

"Kāne'ohe side," he said, draining the last liquid from one can, then popping the top of another. "We building one house for one rich *haole* that stay mainland."

"You still working with Paul?" Mr. Manago remembered when Paul Higata and Winston were little boys running up and down the street between their two houses, both of them barefoot and dark brown from playing in the sun.

"Yeah. And one weird *haole* guy," Winston said, turning the can of beer in his hand. "He listen to opera all day."

Mr. Manago looked up at the clouds banking up in the afternoon sky. "Is Lester Higata still alive?"

Winston nodded. "I think so. Paul never say his father *make*."

"Since they moved to Makiki, I don't keep up."

"Yeah, plenty people move, but Paul still live in his grandmother's house down at the other end of the street. You know, stay by Mrs. Niitani."

"Sure, I remember. Both your *obāsans* take good care of you."

"Yeah, I one lucky guy," Winston said, draining the last of his beer. "Tomorrow Tuesday. You like something from the store?"

"Just the usual, maybe some green apples," Mr. Manago said.

"Okay, if you think of something, call me. The number's still under my grandmother's name. I like opening the book and seeing her name: Helen Nakamura. Just like she still alive, like maybe I can call her up and she can chew me out like she always did. I miss that old lady telling me how worthless I am."

He laughed and walked away through the dappled light, and Mr. Manago thought he saw some of the radiance that used to surround Debby Uyehara cascading off her son. You're a silly old man, he chided himself. Winston Nakamura? He raised his hand to shade his eyes, but as Winston moved away from him, the light grew until he disappeared in the exploding radiance, so bright it could lift a man up and carry him over the slopes of the mountains, covered like cankers with fast food places and rickety apartment buildings, over the houses of the rich, anchored on the cool upper cliffs, to the high peaks at the center of the island where the old gods slept like dragons waiting for their time to come, over them and past the sheer drop of the Windward side, its slopes like pleated green velvet curtains and on into the midnight blue of the sea, deep as the deepest sleep, so deep that when you fell into it you would never wake.

Later Winston tried to remember why he turned back to look at the old man again. Maybe it was like the doctor said, he probably made some kind of sound, but Winston couldn't remember hearing anything. When he reached his yard, he turned and saw the old man still sitting in his chair with his mouth open in a large black circle and his hand clutched to his chest.

The ambulance came in five minutes and the paramedics had him revived, strapped on a gurney and on his way to the hospital. Winston rode with him, because there wasn't anyone else.

"It's a good thing you were there," said the paramedic. "You saved his life."

Winston nodded. What if the beer had brought on the heart attack? All he needed was that prick Roland Manago saying Winston killed his dad. He'd have to call Roland and tell him Mr. Manago was in the hospital. Last time he heard, Roland lived in Sacramento. How many Managos could there be in Sacramento? He thought of Roland Manago's pinched face, wrinkled in the center like *li hing mui* seed. How could Mr. and Mrs. Manago have such a son? Winston's grandmother said just like everything else a tight *okole* skipped generations. Mrs. Manago's father had been just like Roland, the cheeks of his *okole* pinched together so tight he could barely sit down. Maybe Mr. Manago wouldn't die, and then he wouldn't have to call Roland.

Mr. Manago didn't die, but the doctors wanted to keep him in the hospital for observation. The old man must have told them about Roland, because two days later Winston saw him dragging a suitcase from a red Impala parked in the driveway behind Mr. Manago's Toyota pickup. Winston wished he had worked overtime like Paul wanted. If only he had taken five more minutes to put up his tools.

"Suck it in," he whispered to himself and walked over to Roland, who was bent over his huge suitcase, the sweat beading on his forehead, glistening in the bright afternoon light. He didn't look any different, maybe a little rounder, a soft paunch under his white dress shirt.

"Hey, Roland," he said, "it's Winston. You remember?"

Roland let go of the suitcase, straightened his body and turned, his pudgy fingers clutching at the collar of his shirt. Winston saw he wore a wedding ring. What kind of woman would marry Roland Manago?

"Oh, you still live here?" Roland said, nostrils flaring, lips pursed tight as the wallet of old Mr. Kim who lived down the street.

"Yeah, I still here," Winston said, suppressing the urge to punch Roland in the middle of his flat face. The last time he'd seen Roland was right after high school, in black pants and a white dress shirt buttoned at the neck. The years had taught him how to buy clothes but hadn't unpinched his mouth.

Roland stood for a moment, mopping the sweat from his brow with a giant white handkerchief. He folded it, pressing the fold between his thumb and index finger, and put it in his pocket.

"What do you want, Winston?" he finally said, eyes darting around as if following the path of a crazed bird. "They told me you saved his life. Do you want a reward or something?"

Winston turned and walked back to his house through the mango grove, the bright afternoon sun softened and dappled by the leaves overhead. He'd known Roland Manago for thirty-six years, and every time he talked to him he wanted to squash him like a bug. The only thing that kept him from it was who would want to spend life in prison for killing Roland Manago? He got into his truck and drove to the North Shore. The waves weren't breaking, but looking at the sun set over the Pacific made Roland Manago's words seem like the buzzing of a fly.

But he did exist. Every day as Winston left for work, the red Impala sat on the street in front of Mr. Manago's house like a curse. And every day when he returned from work over the Pali, there it would be again, sometimes in the same spot, sometimes parked in between the two houses, right in front of the six mango trees.

"Roland was always peculiar," said Paul Higata. Winston and Paul were sitting on the front steps of Winston's house drinking a beer after work. "Remember that time he asked Lorene Watanabe to dance at the Junior Prom?"

"Jeeze, I forgot about that," Winston said, finishing his beer. "He led her out to the middle of the gym and said, 'Okay, now dance.'" Then he walked away and left Lorene looking at all the other couples through the thick lenses of her glasses, tears steaming them while Roland laughed.

"Too bad he forgot Dennis Hapakuku was Lorene's cousin," said Paul.

Winston nodded. "I've never seen a face so messed up," he said. "Roland's eyes were purple for a month."

Now they were all working construction, while Roland had some fancy job in California. Winston didn't care because Roland was Roland and how could money make up for that?

A week after Mr. Manago's heart attack, Winston came home early because it was pouring in Kāne'ohe. In front of Mr. Manago's mango trees there was a truck that had one of those plastic signs on the door: "Chang's Tree Service." Roland's red Impala was pulled up behind it, and Roland was standing on the curb talking to a Chinese guy with long hair pulled back in a braid. Winston parked his truck and went inside, like he hadn't seen them, but he crouched down and watched them from the window in his grandmother's bedroom. The Chinese guy was pointing toward the mango trees and writing something on a clipboard. Winston could smell the storm coming over the mountains from the other side of the island. The leaves of the mango trees were rustling like nervous schoolgirls. Roland took a piece of paper from the Chinese guy and then drove off in the red Impala.

Winston waited for a minute and then ran outside. *Mauka*, toward the mountains, the sky was dark with thunderclouds. The ginger that covered his front yard was dancing in the breezes the clouds were whipping up, and the papaya trees swayed like old-fashioned hula dancers.

"Hey, man," he shouted at the Chinese guy, who was sitting in his truck. "What's going on?" Winston nodded at the grove of mangoes.

"Who wants to know?"

"I'm a friend of the old guy who owns those trees," Winston said, his hands against the door of the truck. "He's in the hospital."

"Yeah, I was just talking to his son. We're going to take out the trees so he can build a parking lot. You know, so the old man can have some more income."

"You're kidding?" said Winston. "It'll kill him if you cut down those trees."

"It's not my *kuleana*," he said and shrugged. "His son said go ahead." He pulled away from the curb and left Winston standing in the street. The dark rainclouds were racing toward the ocean, hanging low in the sky. The first drops fell on Winston's head and arms. The mango trees stood like six old gods on Lipona Street: not blue-eyed *haoles* like in the Christian churches, but real gods, squat and powerful, as though they had been there before even the first voyagers came to the islands from Tahiti, following the stars in their big dugout canoes.

"Don't be stupid," Winston said to himself, because mango trees weren't native to Hawai'i. They were first planted during the time of Kamehameha I. But in March when the trees bloomed and their red flowers filled the air between his house and Mr. Manago's with their heavenly color, it was as if the islands were once again the paradise that lay undiscovered for so long in the middle of the Pacific Ocean. Winston's grandmother told him that in India the mango blossom was an arrow of the goddess of love. Even Winston Nakamura could see that.

The rain lasted for half an hour or so. When it was over, Winston cut a bunch of red and yellow ginger and drove to the hospital. Mr. Manago was asleep, so Winston sat in the chair by his bed and waited. A pretty *haole* nurse took his flowers and brought them back in a blue vase.

"They smell like heaven," she whispered and put them on a table by the window. No one was in the other two beds in the room. Winston wondered how tall she was. Six feet? He really liked big girls. He was daydreaming about the nurse when Mr. Manago awoke.

"Oh, it's you, Winston," he said, as if he had been dreaming, and Winston Nakamura had not been one of the characters in his dream. Well, Mr. Manago hadn't been in Winston's daydream either, so they were even.

The old man's face was shrunken, like one of those heads Winston saw on a TV show about tribes in South America. His arms were skinny and the flesh hung from the bones. Slowly he pushed himself up in bed. "Where's Roland?" he asked.

"I don't know," said Winston, biting back all the things he wanted to say. They squirmed in the back of this throat, ugly toads or flying cockroaches wanting to escape into the room like a plague in the Bible.

"He said he was coming by," said the old man. "What's that smell?"

"I brought you some ginger from my grandmother's garden," Winston said. How was he going to bring up the mango trees? The ginger plants were a place to start, but he felt too stupid to figure out how to say what he'd come to say.

"Your *obāsan*'s garden," Mr. Manago said. "I was just dreaming about her. She was flying above your house like a little brown bird, only she was wearing that blue and white muumuu. You know, the one with the plumerias. It was so funny to see a bird wearing a muumuu."

"Roland going cut down the mango trees," Winston said and closed his mouth fast, as if one of those warty toads had hopped across his tongue and landed on the white hospital blanket that covered Mr. Manago's skinny legs.

"What did you say?" the old man asked.

Winston repeated his statement.

"Oh, that's what he's been talking about. I couldn't really understand what it was. My brain's not so good since the heart attack. I hear the words but I don't know what they mean."

Winston leaned in closer to Mr. Manago. The antiseptic smell of the room collided with the heady scent of the ginger. His stomach turned over like a boat on choppy water.

"He had one guy out today looking at your trees."

"He thinks I need more money," said Mr. Manago, "but I tell him I have plenty. The house is paid for, and I have my government check."

"You better tell him not to do it," Winston said, his voice rising. His friend nodded, but it was if he were barely in his body. His eyes were glassy and dull like the clouded windows of the hospital room.

Roland walked into the room, his head like a big cabbage. "Tell me what?" asked Roland, his thick lips moist and red.

Mr. Manago stared straight ahead as if watching a TV show on the blank wall of the hospital room.

Winston stood up. He was a little guy but he was taller than Roland Manago, and he was tougher. All his years working construction had made his body sinewy and strong. Roland looked like a big soft *mochi* ball.

"You no can cut down the mango trees," Winston said.

Roland stood at the end of his father's bed and tucked the blanket under his feet. "It's none of your business, Winston."

"Yes, it is. You cut down those trees, going kill your dad."

"I don't think so. We're being practical here, right, Dad?"

Mr. Manago's gaze focused and he nodded.

Winston put his face right in front of Mr. Manago's. "He going cut down your trees."

Mr. Manago looked around Winston's head to where Roland was standing at the end of the bed. "I'm an old man, Winston. He's my son."

A slow smile spread over Roland's face, a smile Winston had seen before, a smile like a lizard crawling on a sunny wall an inch away from a juicy bug.

"You not old," said Winston. "You can live plenty more years. What you going to do without your trees?"

Mr. Manago closed his eyes. He looked like a skeleton on the bed. One of his feet had escaped from the covers. The long yellow toenails glowed under the fluorescent light like the skin of some prehistoric fruit.

"It's over, Winston," said Roland. "Leave before I call the police. If he has another heart attack, I'll sue you and take everything you have, even that beat-up old pickup truck. I'll take your house, tear it down, and pave it over, too."

Winston drove *ewa* on H1 until Farrington Highway ended in Wai'anae and drove on till the road ended at Yokahama Beach. He turned around and parked at Makaha and swam out into the Pacific until he could think of something other than Roland Manago's face. His arms ached and he turned and looked back toward the island. The mountains reared up in the distance like the breasts of a beautiful goddess beckoning him to come back. The water stung his eyes and his mouth was full of salt. All the ugly things he wanted to say were gone. He swam back to shore, and sat on the beach. Two *haole* girls were lying on a blanket, listening to music through headphones. A group of boys was bodysurfing, their voices floating over the swells of the ocean.

Winston didn't kill Mr. Manago. He died a week later, the day the Chinese guy and his crew cut down the mango trees and pulled the stumps out of the ground with winches and chains. The crew filled in the holes and then poured black asphalt over the lot. It looked like the lava fields on the Big Island, black and hard and smelling of sulfur.

After the funeral, Roland flew back to Sacramento. The lawyer sent someone to clear out the house. Winston walked over while they were working and asked what they were going to do with the photographs. The fat *haole* woman in charge of the cleanup said they were sending the furniture over to Goodwill, but they usually just threw the photos away. Nobody wanted someone's old pictures. Winston asked if he could buy the Managos' photographs.

"They were good friends with my grandmother," Winston said. "Could be some photos of her."

The woman shrugged. "You can have them. Those two boxes over there," she said, pointing to the brown plaid couch under the living room window.

Winston lugged the boxes back to his house. It was a couple of weeks before he got around to going through them. One rainy Saturday after Thanksgiving he found what he was looking for— a photo he'd taken of Mr. Manago a few years before, sitting under his mango trees on an afternoon much like the last one when they had shared the beers. He took the photo down to the copy shop on Varsity and had three blowups made, one for each window that overlooked the parking lot where Mr. Manago's mango trees once stood. He taped one to the kitchen window, one to the bathroom window, and one to the window of his grandmother's bedroom. Not that he believed in ghosts or anything like that, but just in case the old lady was still around.

They sold Mr. Manago's house right away, but nobody wanted the lot. The new neighbors put up a fence so they wouldn't have to look at the asphalt cracking, tough green weeds breaking through, fed by the cow manure. Winston swore one day he would save enough money to buy the lot, tear up the asphalt and replant the six mango trees, but how could Winston Nakamura save that much money? After all, he had barely finished high school while Roland Manago had gotten a scholarship and now had a big job on the mainland, counting the money of people he would never see.

The
Li Hing Mui
Fiasco
1986

My name is Winston Nakamura. I never know why I do this. I no can write, but when I seen Lani yesterday at Makapu'u, I start thinking about her brother Chris again. She had some kids with her, so I guess she married. Man, I feel sorry for her husband and the poor kids, too. She like make pretend she never know me, but I went right up to her and said, "Hey, sistah." She said, "Oh, hi, Winston. How you doing?" We went talk little bit, you know—*howzit, where you stay?* But her eyes like two Ping-Pong balls, looking at the sky, the kids, the beach, everything but me. Pretty soon she tell the kids they got to go, and they went drive off in a beatup VW, you know, the kine with no top. She never said nothing about Chris.

I know Chris from small-kid time. I live with my grandmother on Lipona Street in the green house with all the papaya trees. I still stay there. The old lady really like papayas. She say that's why she get so old, eating plenty papayas and the mangoes from Mr. Manago's yard next door. Chris live down two streets. We do everything together: play tetherball, surf, throw eggs at cars on H1. We go to Takahashi Store on Beretania for crack seed, not the dry *manini* ones in the plastic bag but the big juicy wet ones old Mrs. Takahashi used to scoop out of glass jars the size of one small TV. Takahashi Store stay close to where we live on Lipona Street. Mr. Takahashi is *make-die-dead*, but nobody fool with the old lady cause she got one gun under the counter. One day she almost shoot off Milton Hong's arm for trying to steal one pack Juicy Fruit. She one crazy old lady.

My grandmother tell me *li hing mui* means "traveling plum." In olden times they give the Chinese soldiers salted plums cause they last one long time, like for when they go to war or whatever. She Japanese so I ask how she know all this kine Chinese stuff. She say she know plenty more than I think, like what me and Chris been smoking in the hedge behind Mr. Manago's house. That stupid suckup Roland Manago. Man, I like go kill that guy. Always sneaking round, spying on everybody with one face like one flat shovel.

I like *li hing mui* okay, but my favorite is shredded mango. I could eat that stuff till I puke. But Chris he love the wet *li hing mui* more than anything. All through grade school we go to Taka-hashi Store for soda and crack seed, you know, cause we got nothing better to do. Coach want Chris to play baseball, but he too cool for that shit. He say, "Why I like stand around and hit one little ball with one stick?" Chris is like that, but fun, you know. Then everything change.

One day we go to the store, like always, and we see that stupid *moke* Bollie Nishigawa and his three friends. I never know their names. Bollie one nasty-looking guy. Even though it stay hot, he wear one big corduroy jacket, dark brown, which mean he sniff-ing. You know, they cut the lining and in the arm hide the glue, whip it open, then sniff it up so the teachers and nobody else can see them. But who wear one big jacket in Hawai'i? Gluesniffers.

Everybody knows, but glue sniffing no make you smart, and Bollie one stupid gluesniffer.

Bollie got one thin little mustache like the hair on the stomach of one old dog. Chris's sister Lani stay with him, and Bollie feeling her up, you know his hands all over. She only twelve but she still got one body, little boobs and one high *okole.*

Lani went look at Chris, half shame and half what-you-going-do-about-it? Bollie is fifteen, just like us. He went see that look and run his hand under her shirt, rubbing the skin of her back just like he own her or something. Chris just stand there staring at Bollie.

Right away, I got to say. Something wrong with Lani. Even when she was little she was weird, kapakahi, you know? All through high school she got one reputation. I mean she'd do it with anybody. She even come on to me, but hey, man, I think too much about germs. Plus, she Chris's sister.

Anyway, Bollie say, "What you staring at, bruddah?"

Chris never say nothing, but all the time he staring at Bollie's hand rubbing up and down under his sister's blue shirt like waves in the ocean, though I never seen nothing in the ocean as nasty as Bollie Nishigawa's chewed-on glue-crusted fingers.

"Come on, Lani," Chris finally say. "We go home."

"Why," say Bollie, "so your father can get his turn?"

This was when Chris plowed into Bollie, like one tank knocking over one weed.

If you never see him then you don't know, but Chris one big guy. He *hapa*—part Hawaiian, part *haole.* Chris and Lani's father went come from the mainland right after the war. Maybe he was in the navy or something. Even the ugliest *haole* can marry one Japanese, Chinese, or Hawaiian girl, and have good-looking kids. I never know what it is. Chris's mother is Ruby Kaapuni, half Hawaiian, half a lot of other things. His sister, Lani, stay good looking, I guess, but too skinny for me. Even though I one shrimp, I like the big girls. Man, those giant Samoans make me *lōlō,* but I too chickenshit to go out with them anymore after Yvonne Tafeaga went almost smother me when she passed out on top me. Anyway, Chris is one big, good-looking guy. Hey, I not one *mahu* or anything, but I no can help notice all the girls dying for him even though we freshmen. Senior girls, brah. It was great for me, because they go out with me just cause I'm his friend. Wendy Kobayashi and Laverne Peterson, even they go out with me. Only one date, sure, but I felt up Laverne. Man, she had big tits. When we go high school, I think maybe Chris never like be friends with me. I was wrong. He still hang with me.

So Bollie is in big trouble with Chris on top of him. I stand back and let him show his stuff. Even Bollie's friends never want to mess with Chris. He's on top of Bollie, punching his ugly face when I see something come from behind, something fast and black. It's Lani with one metal pole she pick up in the lot next to Takahashi Store. She hit Chris one time on the head before I grab her around the shoulders and drag her off, screaming like one animal, like the mongoose I saw near my uncle's place in Waialua. A car hit him and he made this sound like the world was over and everything was suck down his throat. It's too much. Lani going hit Chris again if I never stop her.

Bollie screaming, too, cause he like one little bug pinned under Chris. Bollie's friends push Chris off and run away, stupid chickenshits. Lani keep dancing round Chris screaming and pulling her hair.

Finally Mrs. Takahashi come out. "You kids fighting? I going call the police."

"Call one ambulance, old lady. This guy *make*."

When Lani hear me say *make*, she yell even louder and run down the street. I still get the pole she hit Chris with waving it over my head. "Killer. I going tell them what you did. Killer."

I think Chris is *pau*. The ambulance comes screaming up Beretania, and the medics swarm round Chris like flies on shredded mango. He never move, so I said, "He *make*, right?"

"Nah," said the *haole* guy. "He's breathing, but he's not going to be catching waves anytime soon." They strap Chris to a rolling bed and take him hospital. I went call his mother, but she too drunk to know what I'm telling her. Finally, I say, "Ask Lani what happen," and hang up.

Chris is out for three days. I sit in the hospital room with his mother and grandmother. You can see where Chris and Lani get their looks. Ruby Kaapuni still look like one movie star, even half-drunk and too fat. Her mother, Hannah Kaapuni, is Hawaiian, too. She one tall, silent lady, who know all the old stories and songs. Man, I love to hear her sing in Hawaiian, her voice deep as one man. When we was little kids, me and Chris went put my pup tent in the backyard and sleep there all summer, looking at the stars and listening to his grandmother sing on the lanai.

Chris's father never come see him even one time at the hospital. Wasn't one secret Lani was his favorite. He treat Chris like one slave. He buy plenty houses all over O'ahu and fix them up and rent them. He always working on one house and lots of times he take Chris with him to help. I go, too. That's how I learn to be one carpenter. Chris's father know everything about building one house and fixing it up. He one good teacher.

"Winston, you have a knack for carpentry," he say in his flat *haole* voice, black hair standing up like one rooster. He one quiet guy but sometimes he go wild and lose it all over the place. One time he went chase Chris down the street screaming, "I'm going to kill you when I catch you." He no catch him that time, but he did plenty till Chris was big enough to beat him up and then *pau*. He never touch him again.

The police never did nothing to Lani, I guess cause she only twelve. When Chris wake up from the coma he say his spirit went sit in the corner of the hospital room on top the TV set. It was on all the time so Ruby and her mother can watch soaps and *The Price Is Right*. Chris say he sit on the TV and stare at his body in the bed.

"What you look like?" I ask him.

"Like one kalua pig with dead pig eyes."

"Why you come back?"

"I couldn't help it, man. My body was calling me."

It was Chris who told me that *haole* mean ghost. When the Hawaiians on Kaua'i first saw Captain Cook's men, they thought they was from the land of the dead. His grandmother tell him this story about an old-time Hawaiian dude who was hurt bad. So his spirit leave his body through his eye and went fly until he came to one big field where plenty spirits were wrestling, gambling, eating at one *lū'au*. One lady tell this dead guy's spirit he can go back inside his body but no fool with any spirits or take anything back with him. If he do, he live in the land of ghosts forever. This guy want to stay in the spirit world, I guess, cause they having so much fun. But this lady keep him straight. They went back to his house, and she went push him back into his body.

"When I was out, I go to the spirit world," Chris said. "Before I come back, I grab one piece of grass and try swallow it. Getting back in your body is pretty hairy. I never know if I swallow it or not."

But later, I know Chris swallow that piece of grass. He breathing, eating, farting, just like anybody, but he's in the land of ghosts, too.

Chris change. How? This is hard. He still one great guy, but he act all funny kine, you know, like something eating him. And he never want to do nothing—catch some waves, go to the beach, smoke a little weed, nothing. For two years I go down to his house, and we watch TV. He never even pick out the show. We just watch what Ruby and his grandmother watch. Their favorite is *Dark Shadows*, this show about vampires. Chris's mother in love with the head vampire Barnabas. She talk about him like he one real person. I mean I know she drink plenty, but jeeze, is just TV. Sometimes I think about if the stories Chris's grandmother tells could be on TV, so everybody could know about the old ways, like if you could see what the islands were like before Captain Cook and the missionaries. Of course, no sugar cane or pineapple, so no Japanese coming to Hawai'i to work in the fields. Too bad for me, but anything is better than those vampires or guessing how much one washing machine cost.

So one day when Chris come to my house and say, "Hey, brah, you want go to the store?" I surprised.

"For what?" I say.

He look at me funny kine and say, "You know, for crack seed."

I say, "Whatever," but we never do this since tenth grade when he went fight Bollie Nishigawa, and Lani went crack his head with one pipe. I never say nothing, just get in the car, an old rusted-out Chevy that belong to his grandmother.

I guess I was looking at him funny, cause he say, "I owe you money, or what?"

"No, man, but I no like crack seed. I want one plate lunch or something."

He never listen to me. He say, "I got to get out of here," and look up at the sky. I never know what he mean.

"Where you like go? Big Island?"

"No, man, mainland."

I never know what to think. We was driving down King Street. He hang a left and pull up in front of Takahashi Store. We get out of the car and when we go inside he say to me real quiet, "Keep talking to the old lady."

What? But we already in the store, and Chris ask can he use the bathroom. The old lady see him a million times so she nod her head. I never know what to do so I start talking. "How the shredded mango?"

"How you think it is?" she say. "Same as always, red and sweet."

She the same as always. Old and crabby.

"Yeah, but it look more red than before."

She give me stink eye. "You want some, or what?"

"Yeah, but give me some wet *li hing mui*." She walk over to the big glass jars and start scooping some out in one little bag.

"Hey, too much, already."

She shake her head and put the lid back on the jar. She twist the bag and say, "One quarter," and stick out her hand. It look like one branch from one old tree with her veins all knotted up under her brown skin.

I dig around in my pockets but no more nothing. I pull out the pockets. Pukas in both.

I look up and Chris is right behind us.

"Hey, brah," I say. "You got one quarter?"

His eyes look funny kine. He give me the money, and I give it to Mrs. Takahashi. Her hands snap around the quarter like one poi dog eating a steak.

Chris already outside. The car is running and before I can even close the door Chris driving away.

"Hey, man, slow down." Then I see the gun in the front seat between us. Unreal! "What is that?"

"Cool it, Winston."

"That's Mrs. Takahashi's gun."

He stop the car in the middle of Beretania Street. "Get out."

"Why, man?"

"It's my *kuleana*."

His *kuleana*. I'm walking home in the rain. Why is it his *kuleana*? Why he want to go shoot his father and mother? I never know. Everybody say was acid or something like that, but I seen him right before, and I no think so. Ruby was okay. Chris only hit her in the leg, but the father *make*. Lani went stay with her auntie in LA. She never come back for two years. Her mother sell the house on Lipona Street and move Kāne'ohe side. I never see Lani till at Makapu'u the other day.

They never put Chris in jail. He went hospital in Kāne'ohe. I went see him two or three times, but he so doped up was like talking to one bowl of poi. Couple of years later somebody say they let him out, that he was preaching down Waikīkī. I went and seen him, walking up and down by Liberty House, yelling about God and Satan and evil and all that shit. I never even talk to him. The Chris I know was gone.

I stay in my grandmother's house now and work construction. She *make* a few years before, but her papaya trees still doing good. I work in the yard just like when she was there. Sometimes I surf, drink a few beers, smoke a little weed. The break at Sandy's big this week, so I never go work. After Chris was in the papers, all the girls go out with me cause I'm his friend. They want to talk about what happened, but then they forget about him. I never forget. At Makapu'u I should have asked Lani some things like: Where your brother? Where my friend, sistah? Where I going get another friend like that?

Linda Higata's Room 1982

When Mei Lan Hee was kidnapped it was front page news, but right away everyone on Lipona Street thought something was fishy. Mei Lan had married a doctor, but she wasn't that rich. Mr. and Mrs. Chiu, her mother and father, never left the old neighborhood even when H1, the freeway that cut through Honolulu like a jagged scar, gobbled up houses two blocks away. Sure, Mei Lan and Thomas Hee had a house in Hawai'i Kai, but they bought it before the real estate boom of the eighties, which knocked so many local people out of the market.

All the aunties in the neighborhood told Mrs. Chiu she was lucky her daughter married a doctor. Mrs. Chiu nodded, but the aunties could tell she thought luck had nothing to do with it. Hard work had landed that surgeon, Mrs. Chiu's hard work and, of course, Mei Lan's. After Mr. Chiu died of a heart attack while using the pressing machine, Mrs. Chiu had slaved on in their drycleaning store in Nu'uanu day after day to send their son Douglas to Punahou and Mei Lan to St. Andrew's Priory. Now Douglas was a pediatrician in Oakland, and Mei Lan had gone to nursing school at UH and met Thomas Hee while she was working as a surgical assistant at Queen's Medical Center. Mei Lan wanted to work with children, but old Mrs. Chiu said that she would have better luck if she went into surgery. A mother always knows what's right for her daughter.

"She's dead," said Miriam Oh, when they first read the news in the *Advertiser*.

"Oh, Auntie," said Linda Higata, "don't say that."

This wasn't simply superstition on Linda's part. Mrs. Oh had no little reputation on Lipona Street as a woman who could see into the future. She had predicted the death of the *haole* boy down the street, and she had seen the death head over Ruby Kaapuni's husband. That's what she called it, the death head, but when questioned, Miriam confessed that it was like a little cloud of dark brown smoke, hovering over the head of someone who would soon die.

Miriam Oh shrugged and lit another cigarette, perfect dragon-lady red fingernails hovering around her lacquered crash-helmet bouffant of jet black. Before she retired, Mrs. Oh had been a beautician, but she still did the hair of her friends. She was always trying to give Linda a perm, but Linda thought that any Japanese woman, even a half-Japanese woman, under sixty with curly hair was trying to look like a grandmother.

Holding up the paper, Linda's mother, Katherine Higata, said, "They found all her rings under the front seat of her car. She must have known something was happening, to hide those rings." Her blue eyes were focused on the newspaper with the kind of concentration necessary for surgery or freeing hostages in the grip of psychotic terrorists.

"That is so Chinese," said Mrs. Nagoshi, the Higata's mousy neighbor two houses down the street. "I would have said, Here, take the rings."

"How would you know?" snapped Miriam Oh, taking a long

drag on her cigarette and flashing her star sapphire set in baguette diamonds.

Mrs. Nagoshi looked down at her own hands and her wedding band, cheap and too small since she had gained so much weight.

Linda's mother cut in. "The kidnappers must have been pretty stupid if they thought a doctor's wife didn't wear at least one big diamond."

Mrs. Higata was from Ohio. She had been a nurse during World War II and met Lester Higata at Tripler. Wounded in Germany, he was in Tripler for rehabilitation on his bad leg. She told Linda that as far as her mother was concerned, she might as well have married a black man. Linda remembered the one time that her grandmother had come to visit. She was an old *haole* woman, but you could tell that she had been beautiful once. Linda and her parents and brother had gone to the dock to pick up the old lady and her husband. Mrs. Higata's round blue eyes had been filled like the bowls of water in which they floated orchids. She kept saying, "Mama, Mama, Mama," until her mother snapped, "That's enough, Katherine. Introduce me to my grandchildren."

"Have they heard from the kidnappers yet?" Linda asked. She remembered Mei Lan in her nurse's uniform and pink mohair sweater walking down Lipona Street to the bus stop.

"Forty thousand dollars," said Miriam Oh with disgust. "I'm telling you, she's dead. Only amateurs would ask for such a *manini* ransom. When they see the trouble they're in, they'll kill her."

"We have to call her parents," said Helen Nagoshi.

Everyone in the room was silent.

"Helen," Mrs. Higata said, "remember we went to Mrs. Chiu's funeral last year?"

Mrs. Nagoshi teared up, "I didn't forget. So many died last year. My Wesley." Last March the police had found Wesley Nagoshi crumpled up in an alley in Waikīkī, dead from a heroin overdose.

Mrs. Higata put her arms around the little woman and patted her back. "Here, let me pour you some more coffee."

Linda looked at her mother and wondered how she did it. She could calm anyone with the simplest words and just a little pat. Linda wished she could do half as much for her patients. All she usually did was nod her head through one heartbreaking story after another. In fact, lately she found herself becoming unimpressed by mere heartbreak. It took something more, something really hideous, to shake her out of her stupor.

Miriam Oh sniffed. "Linda, when are you going to marry a doctor?"

"I am a doctor, Auntie," Linda said, with as much hope of being heard as a violin in the roar of a tidal wave.

"I'm talking about a man." Miriam Oh crushed her cigarette in the saucer of her coffee cup.

"Men are scarce."

Miriam rolled her eyes, lit another cigarette, and through a cloud of smoke said, "They are nonexistent."

"I wouldn't say that, but definitely scarce. I made a strategic error not getting married in my twenties. Oh, well," she said and shrugged.

"What about Mark?" asked Mrs. Nagoshi.

Mark was Linda's *haole* boyfriend. He taught English at Roosevelt High and edited a literary magazine, *Mango Tilt!* Mark and Linda had been going together for eight years.

"I think we know each other too well."

"What's that supposed to mean?" snapped her mother.

Linda didn't really know what she meant. She put her arm around her mother and laughed. "Too bad you already have a husband, because you and Mark would make a great couple."

Mrs. Higata pushed her daughter away. "You're a bad girl." Linda's mother was crazy about Mark. They were both news hounds and could sit around and discuss the fine points of controversial trade agreements and social legislation, Mrs. Higata on the right and Mark on the left. Linda's mother still thought Nixon was misunderstood.

"Why don't you two run for office?" Mr. Higata once asked.

"Daddy, they would have to run against each other, and then where would we be? All our secrets would be on the front page of the *Advertiser*."

"You're right, girlie. I'd better shut up."

"What about your new boyfriend, Auntie?" Linda asked. This marriage talk was not a topic that ever worked out to her advantage.

"He's good looking and a terrific dancer, but he has an eye on my money."

"So what? He's not going to get anything from you."

"No, but when he figures that out, it's over." She sighed. "He knows how to dress," she said like a little girl thinking about a chocolate ice cream cone.

When Linda was a teenager she had asked Auntie Oh why she wasn't psychic when it came to her own life. "Because," she said, "I can only see myself in a mirror and that's not real seeing. You know, I couldn't tell if anything was going to happen to Kennedy, and I saw him on TV just before Dallas. That's not seeing either. I have to see the person. It doesn't work for me. I get feelings about what I should do, but sometimes I don't pay attention. What I want is stronger than what I feel."

Helen Nagoshi stood up. "I have to be going. You know, dinner."

"Bye, Auntie," Linda said, as the little woman waddled out the door like a sad duck trailing her white feathers behind her.

"Is she fat," said Mrs. Oh, as soon as Mrs. Nagoshi had shut the door.

"Miriam," Linda's mother said in a loud whisper. "She'll hear you."

Miriam Oh shrugged. "It's the truth."

Linda stood up. "I should be going too. I'm meeting Mark for dinner."

"Where are you going?" asked her mother.

"That new Italian place on Kapi'olanī."

Linda held her breath. Now her mother would talk about how great Mark was, how handsome, how much fun, how Linda should marry him. He was going to get away. Someone was going to snap him up, take him away from Linda. But she didn't. The look passed over her blue eyes, like a movie that Linda had seen so many times she could repeat whole scenes from memory. Katherine Higata closed her blue eyes and said nothing.

When Linda was a girl, she had been obsessed by her mother's eyes, so different from her own, her brother's, and her father's. When she was six, she asked her mother if the world was lighter through pale eyes. Mrs. Higata had laughed and said, No, it's the same. But Linda thought about it for years. How could it be the same? Sometimes she'd take off her sunglasses and look out at Honolulu, blinded by the brilliant sun and think, This is how my mother sees the world. Linda put her Honda into reverse. Her mother was right. Mark was great. She should marry him. Mark was great. Great. Fun. Great fun.

At least her mother wasn't talking about her eternal soul. This was a far more uncomfortable subject for Linda than whether or not she would marry and take her rightful place in the world as a mother and general household slave. About once a year, Mrs. Higata would ask Linda, "Do you ever think about your eternal soul?" Of course, Linda could never admit that she often thought about her eternal soul. It was one of the many things she found irritating about having been raised in the church—the habit of metaphysical thought.

She drove down Beretania, turned left on McCully to Ala Wai, and drove around for twenty minutes until she found a spot by the canal. When she was a teenager, parking in Waikīkī had been easy, but nothing was easy now. There were too many cars, too many people from the mainland with no links to the islands. Ordinary people couldn't buy a house. Oh, well, trouble was good for a psychologist, she thought, watching the trade winds ruffling the palms. She sat in her car for a few minutes and thought about going back to her office. Mrs. Thompson had left her a pile of insurance forms to sign, and she could look over her notes for tomorrow's group. Instead, she got out of her car, locked it and walked up Seaside, turned left and climbed up a flight of stairs and knocked on an apartment door.

The door opened as if on its own, and Linda walked into a dim room, thin slats of bright light breaking through the jalousie windows. He grabbed her from behind. She twisted around to face him.

"You never scare me," she said before he kissed her.

"I don't want to scare you. I can't wait to get my mitts on you."

"Mitts?"

"The body part that goes into mittens."

"A cold weather reference." Linda looked at this man's face as if she hadn't been looking at it for the past year and a half. She pushed his light brown hair back from his face. "I've never seen snow." This was a lie. When she had been a graduate student at UCLA, she and her boyfriend had spent many weekends at Lake Tahoe where his family had a house.

"It's not that terrific, especially after four months and the sky dark at four in the afternoon." He was from Chicago.

She was going to tell him that she had almost not come to the apartment, but what was the point? She had locked her car and made the short walk and here she was. Why quibble over the gray area of volition? She hated it when her patients did it.

As if reading her mind, he said, "I was worried that you wouldn't come," leading her down the hall to the bedroom.

"Why?"

"I can sense you're getting tired of this," he said.

The bedroom was plain, a brown and white tapa print spread over the bed and a green painted chest of drawers.

"Tired of this?" she asked. She shook her head and unbuttoned his shirt. This was the only thing she wasn't tired of, this little cave of a room with the jacaranda tree shading the louvered windows. The rest of her life tired her, but it was her real life and this was nothing.

Later when she was getting dressed, Linda was surprised by her face in the steamy bathroom mirror, the way her father and mother were both present like a double exposure. She didn't really look Japanese, though the Japanese was apparent. Yet there was her mother, too, the wide eyes and the square jaw of Ohio.

"What are you doing tonight?" he asked. He was lying on the bed with his head propped on a folded pillow.

"Why do you want to know?" She noticed that he hadn't put on his shoes. She loved to look at his feet. They were small for such a tall man and lightly freckled.

"I like to think about you and what you are doing. It makes it easier to go home and do the things I have to do."

She shrugged. "I have a patient to see, and then I'm going out to dinner."

"With Mark?"

"No, the Ayatollah Khomeini." She brushed her hair out of her eyes.

"He's dead."

"He came back to life just to go out with me."

"Where are you going?"

"I don't know," she lied. "Somewhere that doesn't serve liquor."

He was baffled.

"Muslims don't drink." She looked around the room for her skirt and found it under the chair. It was black and a little short. She still looked good in short skirts.

"Don't you want to know what I'm going to be doing?" he asked, still lying on the bed.

"Not particularly." Though she had heard many people confess their deepest doubts and secrets, Linda always marveled at how differently men's and women's minds worked. Why would she want to picture him with his wife and children? Even thinking about it was painful.

"Do you ever think of me?" he asked.

She stood and looked at him and tried to pretend that she had never seen him before. Who was he? What was she doing in this room with him? In a sense it was mysterious.

"No," she said, because she knew she thought of him much more than he did of her.

"I didn't think so." She could tell she had hurt his feelings even though he knew she was lying.

"Well, you were right." She was on her knees, searching for her sandals. This was where it got complicated. Although she loved him more than he loved her, she got to act as though she didn't care and he got to act hurt. Or maybe one of them wasn't acting. Or both.

"I think they're in the other room."

She stood and walked through the doorway and saw her sandals in the middle of the floor. She slipped them on, easing the straps over her heels with her toes.

"Where are your shoes?" she called, glancing around the room.

"In here."

She walked back to the doorway. "I have to go." She smiled.

"I tried to call you this afternoon."

"Oh, I went to visit my mother. She was upset. That woman who was kidnapped used to live on our street."

He sat up. "I know them. Melissa worked on some committees with her. The Heart Association and Punahou."

He always spoke of his wife as if Linda knew her, as if they were friends and had lunch together. She had seen them once at Ala Moana. His wife was slim and had straight blonde hair and beautiful legs.

She nodded and slung her handbag over her shoulder. "I have to go." She kissed him, turned and left. This was the hardest part for her, leaving the small dark apartment and walking out into the bright sunshine. She felt like a novice leaving her convent, leaving her pure life devoted to God and walking out into the bright sinful world, not an analogy that held up very well if you thought about it for more than a few seconds.

She counted the steps to the corner, and then counted the steps to Ala Wai Boulevard. One hundred and seventy-two. She unlocked the door of her car. For some reason the palm trees against the metallic blue sky made her think of the story of Lot's wife in the Bible. Though unwilling to make a connection with her present circumstances, she didn't look back.

The office was stuffy when she arrived. She opened the windows and turned on the ceiling fan. Mrs. Thompson had taken off early but had left the coffee machine ready. One of her children was visiting from the mainland, and she wanted to be at the airport to meet him. She had four children. The oldest girl was about Linda's age and was an attorney in Seattle, and the youngest was an elementary school teacher in Florida. The middle daughter was a mess, though Mrs. Thompson didn't talk about her much. Once the middle daughter had come by with her little girl. She was a big talkative woman, someone who would have a lot of acquaintances and not many close friends. Her first words to Linda were, "You need to jazz this place up." The daughter, Carol, was wearing lime green leggings and a silver and black striped top. Her hair was in a bun on the back of her head, a ball point pen stuck through the knot of hair. Mrs. Thompson rushed her out before she could make any more observations.

Linda clicked on the coffee machine and sat down in one of the soft gray chairs and read her notes from last week's session.

Ken Kobayashi lived with his mother in Kailua. He and his girlfriend, Tammy Morikawa, had been engaged for ten years, but they couldn't get married because of his mother. She couldn't live alone, and the house was too small for three people. Ken was an architect. Everyone said, build an addition to the house for Mrs. Kobayashi. Ken considered that idea for two years. He drew up the plans, showed them to everyone he knew, got their suggestions, but when he showed them to his mother, she grunted and said that it was her house. Ken and Tammy could move into the *manini* apartment if they wanted to, but she was staying right there in the house that her husband had bought her in 1956, thank you very much. All his friends had encouraged Ken to get married and move into the apartment or better yet Tammy's place. But there had been a rash of burglaries in the neighborhood, kids whose parents worked and left them alone in the afternoons. Mrs. Kobayashi said she was afraid to live alone.

One afternoon at the apartment, Charles had asked her at what age was divorce hardest on children. That was his name: Charles.

"It depends on the child and the parents."

"Generally speaking, though, is it harder if you wait?"

"If the parents don't say ugly things about each other, if the custodial parent's lifestyle doesn't plummet, then the younger the better. Young kids are adaptable."

His children were fourteen and sixteen.

"Professionally speaking, I would advise you to stay put. I'm sure your accountant would say the same thing."

Linda closed her notebook. The smell of coffee was drifting around the room. She poured milk into a little pitcher and opened the bag of cookies Mrs. Thompson had left out. Linda had learned a long time ago that people are more civilized when they have something in their stomachs.

Ken arrived right at five-thirty. He rushed in and shut the door behind him.

"Ken," Linda said, "What's up?"

His face was flushed and he was smiling.

"I wanted to come early and tell you. Tammy and I are married."

"Ken." It was all she could think to say. They had been talking about this marriage for the last two years. Linda had been convinced that Ken would die before his mother, who was a healthy woman of fifty-nine.

"I know, I know," he said, pacing around the gray couch across from Linda's chair. "I didn't think I would ever do it, but I went to Tammy's house on Saturday and some guy from work dropped by, and I could tell if I didn't do something he would steal her away from me. I could see it in his eyes. They were hungry for my Tammy. So I said to her, let's get married. On Monday we went to City Hall and did it."

"I thought Tammy wanted a big wedding." Linda sat down in her chair.

Ken sat in his accustomed place on the couch. "After ten years she didn't care."

"What did your mother say?"

"Nothing."

"Nothing?"

"Well, she said I'd be sorry when she fell and died because there was no one there to care about her."

"That's not nothing."

"What can I do?"

"What do you think you should do?"

"Don't do that to me," he said, his face suddenly red and furious.

"Do what?"

Ken jumped up. "Answer my question with a question!" he shouted, starting to stalk back and forth but getting embarrassed and finally just standing there red-faced and unhappy. "I know what to do. I'll check on her, call her every day, make sure she's okay, but I'm going to live with Tammy."

"I think that's great."

"You do?"

Linda nodded.

Ken sat down, looking like a little boy whose bicycle has just been stolen. "I'm happy but it's going to take getting used to."

When Ken left Linda worked at her desk waiting for Mark to call. At six-thirty, the phone rang. Since she was expecting to hear from Mark, she wasn't surprised to hear someone ask, "Do you know Mark Spiegelman?" Though when she said yes, the oddness of the question became apparent to her, and her mouth filled with dread so that the next sentence was no surprise.

"There's been an accident."

"He's not dead," she said. It was not a question. She forced her voice not to rise on the word *dead* and held her breath.

"No, but he's delirious and asking for you. He has a head injury."

She breathed again. "Where is he?"

"Queen's."

"I'll be right there."

Linda tried not to speed on her way to hospital, though her hands were trembling. When she passed Thomas Square on the right, it was already dark, the lights of the concert hall glimmering through the dark overhang of the enormous banyan trees. The last time she saw poor kidnapped Mei Lan Hee was in the concert hall, before seeing Baryshnikov. She was there with Thomas Hee and their daughter who had the duck walk of a fledgling ballerina. If Mei Lan Hee could be dead, then so could Mark.

Linda found herself pleading with God. If he lives, I'll never see Charles again. She didn't believe in God and yet she was speeding down Beretania Street begging him to save the life of a man who two hours ago she would have said she didn't love anymore. She was making bargains with someone to whom yesterday she would not have granted existence.

At Queen's Medical Center she parked and rushed to the emergency room, where she had to sit for ten minutes before they'd let her see Mark. A few minutes after she arrived a group of screaming teenagers swept in, boys bloody and the girls crying. One girl with hair an improbable color of red kept moaning, "Oh, Marsha. Oh, Marsha." A group of orderlies carried the wounded boy into the inner sanctum.

They didn't want to let her see Mark because they were getting ready to sew his head up.

"It's really bloody," the giant Samoan orderly said, shaking his head.

"I have a strong stomach, Rooney," Linda said, reading the name tag on his jacket. "Blood doesn't bother me."

Still shaking his head, he led her into the tiny room. Mark was lying on a table, babbling to himself. She took his hand in hers and brushed his hair out of his face with her other hand.

"Sweetheart," she said, "it's me, Linda."

"Don't let them put me in jail," he said. His eyes were glassy. A thick pad of gauze was soaking the blood that was oozing out of the back of his head.

"Did he have a painkiller?" she asked Rooney, who had turned his massive bulk away from Linda to get something out of a cabinet in the corner of the room.

He nodded and said, "Yeah."

"Don't let them put me in jail, Lindy." Mark's voice was higher now.

She kissed his forehead. "No one's going to put you in jail." She turned to the orderly. "What happened?"

"He ran a stop sign and smashed into a Cadillac. A woman and her daughter."

"Were they hurt?"

"In a Cadillac? Are you kidding? They walked away, but the cops said his car was totaled."

"I don't want to go to jail," Mark moaned.

"Don't pay any attention," Rooney said. "They all think they're going to jail."

"Why?" she asked, but before he could answer, the doctor sailed into the room like the lead schooner in a little armada of two nurses. "Who is she?" he asked Rooney but nodding at Linda. The two nurses stood in the doorway. One was fat and wore a blue scrub suit. The other one was a beautiful Filipina whose eyes glanced around the room like balls in a pinball machine.

"His girlfriend," said the orderly. "She says blood doesn't bother her."

"Right. Blood doesn't bother anyone. That's why there are so many surgeons in the world." He nodded toward the table.

The orderly and nurses turned Mark over on his stomach. A ragged gash about four inches long ran along the back of his skull. Around the gash was ugly white scalp shaved like clear-cut forest around a jagged river.

"I can see his skull," Linda said.

"It must be a hard one," said the doctor, "because the Xray doesn't show any damage."

A tiny moan escaped from somewhere inside of Linda.

"He's lucky," the doctor said.

"Luckier than Dr. Hee's wife," said the fat nurse, handing the doctor a pad of gauze. "I remember when she used to work here."

Linda watched as the doctor's deft stitches closed the gash on Mark's head, resurrecting the veil of skin that hid the skull and its gelatinous cap from the harsh world.

"Any news?" the doctor asked, finishing his seam.

"She's dead," the nurse said as she and the orderly turned Mark over on his back. The nervous Filipina nurse had disappeared.

"They found her?" the doctor asked.

"No," said the nurse, "but I know she is."

Everyone's a psychic, thought Linda.

"How does it look?" Mark asked, groggy from the drugs he'd been given.

"Much tidier," said Linda.

"Have you ever thought of a career in medicine?" the doctor asked Linda. "Not many people can take looking into the human body like that."

"She's a doctor," said Mark.

The doctor, nurse, and orderly stopped and looked at Linda as though she had tricked them.

"I'm a psychologist. The mind's a messy business, too."

The doctor shrugged and turned to Mark. "You can go home now. I'll leave a prescription at the desk. Take it easy for a few days. Don't run any more stop signs."

Later when they were in the car, Mark said, "I'm sorry about dinner."

"Don't be silly," she said, turning onto Punchbowl Street. She was stupidly happy all the way home.

Mark slept most of the weekend. Linda read, made soup, took a long walk. On Sunday she changed the dressing on Mark's head. The stitches crawled up the gash like spiders.

It was not until Monday morning that the police found Mei Lan Hee in the trunk of an old Ford in the parking lot at Makapu'u. Just as Miriam Oh and the fat nurse predicted, she was dead. The kidnappers had left her alive, tied her up with a gag in her mouth, but Mei Lan had struggled so furiously she had choked on the gag and killed herself.

Of the two images Linda couldn't erase, one was of Mei Lan standing at the bus stop on Lipona Street in her white nurse's uniform and pink mohair sweater. If she'd missed that bus or failed calculus or been sick the night she met Thomas Hee, how different her life might have been. She could still have been working with children with leukemia or glomerulonephritis, married to a teacher or lawyer or not married at all. Instead she was curled up in the trunk of a rusted out Ford Fairlane, hands and feet tied, ringless fingers struggling against the plastic cord, looking up at the inside of the trunk as if it were her last sight of the sky. The other image Linda couldn't forget was Mark's head, the slippery red of the veins over the skull, ragged wisps of hair matted with blood.

She and Mei Lan had started out on Lipona Street, waiting for the same buses, working hard in school, doing what their parents wanted or not, thinking of themselves in certain ways, thinking they had explanations, maps. Then one day Linda woke to see the smooth curve of the sky, so smooth it might be metal, and she thought that most things are accidental, as random as birth and death. And the oddest things seemed important—the pink of Mei Lan's sweater, the white of an exposed skull and the bright sky, clear and blue as her mother's eyes.

Lani
Dances the
Zombie Hula
in LA
1978

Lani was standing in the makeup aisle of the Woolworth's in Hollywood. She hadn't eaten in six days, and her hands were shaking like two maracas in the grip of someone on amphetamines. All she wanted to do was buy a lipstick, but her mother Ruby kept singing an old Hawaiian song, begging Lani to dance the hula her grandmother had taught her. Okay, to be honest, her *tutu* was standing beside Ruby, too, gray hair streaming to her waist, and she wanted Lani to sing "Hawai'i Ponoi," which she'd learned in the fifth grade when they'd run away to Wai'anae and lived in the green Quonset hut on Lualualei Homestead Road. Lani wasn't crazy. She knew they were dead, but the voices were so loud she was almost ready to start dancing just to shut them up.

"Mom," Lani hissed through her teeth. "I'm in Woolworth's."
But Ruby kept singing, *Hawai'i ponoi, nana i kou Moi, kalani
ali'i, Ke ali'i.* Sometimes when Ruby showed up, she was fat and
drunk the way she'd been at the end, but usually she was young
and slim in a *holokū* with a plumeria behind her ear and a pikake
lei, ready to dance at one of the hotels in Waikīkī, her hula like
the curl of a wave on a moonlit night, with the Milky Way strung
over the heavens like the tiara of some giant goddess who ruled
Hawai'i before the *haoles* came with their boatloads of blue eyes
and syphillis.

"Lani."

She jumped and dropped the lipstick. It was a guy with bushy
blond curls. He was wearing a plaid shirt and jeans and work boots
that were caked with mud. He bent over and picked up the lipstick
and handed it to her.

"I know you," she said, his face coming into focus like an old
home movie. It was Jimmy Monroe, not that she really remembered him all that well. It was hard to remember anything when
you hadn't eaten in six days and maybe hadn't slept in three.
Jimmy lived on Lipona Street during the sixties with the rest of
the Monroe brood. He was a friend of Lani's brother Chris, before
Chris shot their father and killed him.

"I'm Jimmy Monroe. I lived down the street from you in Honolulu before we moved to 'Aiea."

Talking was good, talking to anyone. It made the voices go away.
Ruby and her mother were fading down the aisle of Woolworth's,
their hips knocking candy bars and tampons off the shelves as
they moved in their own zombie hula.

"I remember," she said, looking down at her bare feet with
dirty ragged nails. How long had she been wearing these jeans?
And her shirt—it had once been blue. Why hadn't Marguerite
said something? She forgot. Marguerite was mad at her. She was
in San Francisco for a week.

"What are you doing here?" Jimmy Monroe said, but he had
followed her gaze and was now looking at her feet, too.

"In Woolworth's?" She put the cleaner foot on top of the other,
not that she was fooling anyone. They looked like the feet of a
homeless person.

"I was thinking more like LA." His face was plain as vanilla ice cream but sweet at the same time. He was just a little taller than Lani, and a little thick around the waist. Lani liked that in a man. She needed something to hold on to, and sometimes a beer belly was all you had in this fucked up world.

"I'm working as a pastry chef." She turned to the lipsticks and picked out another one. Cherry Madness. What kind of name was that?

"I guess no one's worrying about you stealing food."

Lani's head flew around as though one of the dead people had given it a sharp slap. "Who told you I was stealing?"

Jimmy stepped back until he was leaning between the Maybelline and Revlon displays. "Lani, it was a joke. You don't look like you've had a good meal in a long time."

"I eat," she said. "I work in a fucking restaurant. I eat all the time." She bit her tongue. She sounded rough, like a man itching for a fight, but she was a dirty girl, buying lipstick. How did that sound? How did a woman like that sound?

"Don't get mad. It wasn't like I said you were fat. Isn't that why guys get in trouble—saying girls are fat?"

Lani smiled. "So am I fat or thin?" That was something a girl would say, especially a girl who was buying lipstick, not that she was doing that good a job of it.

"Definitely thin. In fact, so thin that I think I'd better take you out for lunch. There's a burger place near here where the shakes are great. What you need is a milkshake."

"Chocolate?" She tried to put the Cherry Madness back in the display case, but she couldn't roll the new tube back and slip in the tube she was holding. *Goddamn it, now even the display cases are conspiring against you,* screamed her father. *It's a plot so you'll have to buy something you don't even want, never mind need.*

"Double chocolate," Jimmy said, taking the lipstick from her and putting it back into the case next to the other tubes.

Jimmy led her past her screaming dead father and out of the icy Woolworth's to a beatup Chevy truck, blue with every piece of junk in the universe in the back. Lani almost couldn't make herself get into the cab, because of the glare of the orange couch in the back.

"Are you moving?" She ran her hand down the orange velvet cushions. It was the ugliest couch she had ever seen, even worse than the mongoose-brown living room set in her *tutu's* house.

"Maybe," he said and opened the door, helping her into the high seat. "I'm tired of LA. I'm thinking about moving to Alaska. They say you can make $10,000 in a couple of months working in a salmon cannery. I want to move back to Hawai'i and buy a little house in Kāne'ohe or Waialua. My sister's husband's in real estate, and he says prices are going to go through the ceiling."

Lani settled into the passenger's seat of the dirty Chevy. Alaska—that was a place she had never thought of going. Canada was the coldest place she'd ever been. She and Marguerite had taken a weekend trip to Vancouver last October. They had eaten dim sum every day for lunch and snuggled up in the hotel room most nights with room service and a bottle of champagne.

Jimmy turned the engine over. It began purring like a big cat at the zoo, a leopard or tiger.

"It sounds like it might make it to Alaska," Lani said as he pulled out into traffic. "You need to ditch that couch though. Everybody knows orange is bad luck."

"What color couch would be good luck?"

"White but it's not really practical when you're thinking about driving a thousand miles."

"It would be gray by Seattle," Jimmy said, his smile like a hibiscus opening after a morning rain.

"And then your luck would be gone," Lani said turning away from him to the broken-down buildings speeding by. Once people ate lunch there or bought magazines, and this was where movie stars had been discovered. You wouldn't find anything now but some broken-down winos or rats. That's the way it went.

Lani didn't need Jimmy Monroe's smile, but maybe she needed his milkshake, so she sat in his dirty truck like the good girl she'd never been and waited for him to take her whereever he was going.

Pretty soon they were in a booth at a little diner on Sunset. Jimmy was eating a burger and fries, and Lani was sipping a chocolate shake as if it had to last her for the rest of the week.

"How's the shake?" he asked, looking at her as if he were some kind of bug collector looking at an especially juicy specimen through a microscope.

"Hey," Lani said, "I know I look bad."

"Are you kidding? You couldn't look bad if you tried. I always had a crush on you back on Lipona Street. I can't believe I'm actually sitting across the table from you. How long have you lived here? I didn't know you were in LA."

Jesus. How was she supposed to answer all those questions? Crush. What was he talking about?

"Can I get some water?" Lani said. The shake was turning sour in her mouth, or maybe it was her mouth that was sour. She reached for a napkin and pretended to wipe her lips while spitting the mouthful of icy chocolate into the napkin while Jimmy turned to signal the waitress.

"You can have mine," he said, pushing his glass across the table to her. "I haven't touched it."

Lani gulped the water like a drowning woman, which, in fact, she was. She knew it, but that didn't mean she could start doing the breaststroke or even float on her back until the lifeguard showed up.

"Hey, you were thirsty," Jimmy said, eating the last of his burger. "Do you want some of these fries?"

Lani felt the ball of water, milk, and ice cream rise in her throat like a hand pushing up from the bottom of the ocean. She bolted back to the rest rooms and threw up in the toilet. The water had been too cold. If she hadn't drunk the water she would have been fine. Why did she eat anything? It was always the same. She sat on the toilet and thought about the trap she was in. Number one: She couldn't get out of the restaurant without walking past Jimmy Monroe, who was sweet, but made her stomach feel as orange as that ugly couch in his truck. Number two: when and if she could get away from him, it was a long walk home, maybe six or seven miles. But she didn't mind walking.

Two months ago she'd left her car on a street in Santa Monica and walked home. It had taken her two days, but she'd gotten sick of being a taxi for her dead family. They piled into that Toyota and yelled and screamed and whined and sang, until she wanted to drive right off a cliff into the ocean. Her father and Ruby had been screaming in the backseat when she parked the car and left it with the key in the ignition. She loved walking because they were old and dead, so she could outpace them—no problem.

But that still left her with Jimmy Monroe. She opened the stall door and looked at herself in the milky mirror over the sink. Even skinny and strung out, she looked good. After all she was Ruby Kaapuni's daughter. Her face was long and narrow like her father's, but she still had Ruby's creamy skin, her dark liquid eyes, and the waterfall of brown hair, Polynesian despite the *haole* taint, despite the Kentucky backwoods boniness of her father. She was surprised she hadn't slept with Jimmy Monroe. She'd done it with so many guys from the neighborhood. One time she'd been at a party and realized she'd had sex with every man there. It wasn't that big a party—maybe seven or eight guys, but it was weird. Well, whatever she'd done in the past, she didn't want him now. Marguerite was taking care of her.

Outside the ladies' room, she stood in the vestibule. She needed a plan to get rid of Jimmy. Maybe if she just walked past him, she could outrun him when she got outside. He'd have to pay the bill, which would give her about three or four minutes. But what if he just threw the money on the table? She wished she'd paid more attention when they'd parked the truck. Raymond Chandler she was not.

Then she saw an alcove at the end of the vestibule—the fire exit—and she didn't break her stride, pushing open the door and running out into the alley behind the restaurant, the fire alarm clanging before the door shut. Lani didn't look back but ran across the hot asphalt of the parking lot, her feet too dirty and calloused to feel the heat rising from the black tar. She ducked behind a hedge of oleander and found herself on a leafy street of small apartment buildings and old bungalows. Running across the street and through another alley between buildings, she hid behind a green dumpster, peeking over the top from time to time to see if Jimmy's truck was coming down the street. After about twenty minutes she found a low bush, and curled up beneath it and watched the light play through the leaves.

Though it started softly, a song of Pele and the other gods began to waft around the bush, her *tutu* singing the way she had when

Lani and Chris were kids and their mother had dropped them off to go on a bender.

> *Mai Kahiki ka wahine o Pele,*
> *Mai ka aina i Pola-pola,*
> *Mai ka punohu ula a Kane*
> *Mai ke ao lalapa i ka lani*
> *Mai ka opua lapa i Kahiki.*

She'd sing them to sleep with old Hawaiian songs. Lani closed her eyes. She didn't want to see her grandmother, but the song filled her like a big bowl of saimin, the noodles soft and warm. She was asleep when Jimmy's truck passed on the street thirty feet away.

The chill woke Lani, and it was dark. What time was it? Eight? Two? She was cold. Rubbing her arms, she sat up and bumped her head on a branch. For a few seconds she thought she was in the backyard of their house on Lipona Street, in the pup tent with Chris, trying to get away from their father beating Ruby, and then the inevitable reconciliation when they would shake the house with their lovemaking—Ruby screaming like a cat in heat. She must have been faking it, but maybe not. Sex was funny. God, that's one thing Lani knew for sure, how you could love and hate a man at the same time, him lying there on top of you, a god one minute and an animal the next.

On the street Lani tried to remember where she was. Oh, right, Jimmy Monroe—he'd probably given up hours ago. She walked toward the sounds of car horns and engines. Jesus, what day was it? Was she supposed to be at work? She had a quarter in her pocket. Maybe she should call the restaurant, but she was afraid that they'd say yes, where are you, the *profiteroles* aren't made, the lemon tart is lemon soup, the *clafoutis* is just a big pile of fresh cherries. Jesus, how long had she slept? It felt like a few hours, but it could have been days or weeks or months. Maybe it had been years. That was it. She was Sleeping Beauty just up from her 100-year sleep. That would be the answer to her prayers. Her father and Ruby would have dropped from Purgatory to Hell in that time, and Lani was sure the schedule was pretty tight in Hell. They wouldn't be out walking the streets on a day pass.

When she got to Sunset, a shiver shot up her spine, and she could feel her own personal posse of zombies coming up behind, the rustle of their feet, the murmur of their voices, each with its own complaint like a trio in an opera by a Bizarro Mozart. As she set off down Sunset, she remembered using flashlights to read Superman comics with Chris while their parents acted out their tawdry opera in the little house ten feet away, beyond the wall of ginger and papaya trees. She was at the corner of Sunset and Sweetzer. It wasn't really that far from her apartment. She'd be there in a couple of hours tops. She loved walking on Sunset. There were so many people that she wasn't scared. The only bad thing was when she passed a restaurant. The smell of the food was like a forearm down her throat, but that was the great thing about being a fast walker. She could race past a restaurant in less than thirty seconds. What did Jimmy Monroe want anyway? Why had she gone with him to that stupid restaurant? A milkshake. For God's sake, she hadn't had a milkshake since she was seven.

Lani was concentrating so hard on outrunning her ghosts that she didn't hear Jimmy Monroe's truck pull up beside her.

"Lani," he called.

She stopped as if frozen by an alien's stun gun, but she didn't look over at him. She could probably run for a while, but what then? She could feel her father rubbing up against her back, hand reaching for her breasts.

"You didn't have to run away."

She stood like a statue on the sidewalk. Why did she have to talk to this idiot? Just because they lived on the same street in Honolulu? Why wouldn't he disappear? If it weren't for her father and mother, she'd make a run for it, but they were surrounding her like the Sioux in an old Randolph Scott movie, only the Sioux had not been shouting, *Run out into the street. You can get away from him. Just run out in front of that car. You won't have to talk to anyone again. Hawai'i ponoi, nana i komoi.*

"Take me home," she said to Jimmy and ran around the car and jumped into the passenger's side of his truck. Boy, that surprised them. Her father, *tutu*, and Ruby were standing on Sunset like a couple of retards on an field trip.

"Where do you live?" he asked.

"Drive, goddamn it. I'll give you directions later."

He gunned the engine and peeled out. She looked back. Ruby, her father, and her grandmother were standing on the sidewalk by the *Whiskey a Go Go,* her *tutu* in a muumuu, strumming a ukulele, like some kind of big fat Hawaiian tourist attraction. Lani slumped back in the truck and closed her eyes. She couldn't keep running and not eating. Marguerite was sick of her, and Lani didn't want to go back to the hospital. They'd just shoot her full of Thorazine, and then she'd be a zombie herself. Half-dead was worse than dead, because you were awake enough to know you were a corpse.

She looked over at Jimmy Monroe. He was staring straight ahead. What could she expect from him? Well, he'd driven around for a couple of hours in his truck looking for her while she took a nap under a bush.

"Listen," she said. "I'm in trouble. If you can't help me, just drop me off at the hospital. I can't eat, I can't sleep, I can't work, I'm hearing voices. I'm going to kill myself if you don't help me."

"What can I do?" he said.

"Take me to Alaska with you."

He looked over at her. She could see the wheels turning behind his vanilla ice cream *haole* forehead.

Lani knew how he felt. Where had that come from? But the more she thought about it the more she liked the idea. Los Angeles was part of her problem, the job at Marguerite's restaurant, the grid system of the streets. It was too easy to get around, and her father and Ruby could follow her trail through the smog. Even though she didn't eat, she gave off this baloney stink that lingered in the heavy metal of Los Angeles. In Alaska the air was clean. She wouldn't leave a trail there no matter how bad she smelled. And she bet the roads were crooked. Those three old farts wouldn't know what hit them. She looked over at Jimmy Monroe driving his Chevy and smiled at his soft face. She could make him want her. She would have to start eating. It was always hard to start again after she'd stopped, but she could do it if she had to.

"Turn left on Doheny," she said. That's what she needed—clean air and some turns in the road. But what about Jimmy? Yeah, he wanted her, but did he need that much trouble in his doughnuts-for-breakfast life? Who did? If he had any sense, he'd run screaming to Alaska and gut salmon until he gathered his stash and was able to hula on back to Oʻahu to buy his little termite shack on the North Shore.

Lani was counting on him being a little stupid about sex. Most men were. She could do that fake hula in her sleep. She could get up in front of the tourists and swing her hips to "Lovely Hula Hands" and make them think they were seeing the real thing. She'd been doing that hula since the first night her father slipped into bed with her, Ruby drunk in some bar in Waikīkī or Kalihi, losing her beauty in the acres of flesh she was building around whatever was left of the Hawaiian girl who met the *haole* officer after the war. Her parents' story was like a fairy tale but one where the witch baked the two kids up good, roasted their tender little asses and served them up with new potatoes, French-cut green beans, and a big three-layer chocolate cake.

When they got to Lani's apartment, she flipped the switch but no lights. Shit, she'd forgotten to pay the bill. Marguerite was going to kill her. Where was her purse? She had seven hundred dollars in her wallet. In the moonlight from the kitchen window, she saw it on the table. She turned at the door and waved him away.

"I'll be okay," she said. "I need to sleep." Fat chance—that nap under the bush was the first time she'd slept in days, which meant she probably wouldn't sleep again until February.

Jimmy was standing on the sidewalk like a mendicant friar, his hands clasped in front, legs planted about a foot apart. Or maybe he was a paramilitary operative standing ready to storm her fortress. Lani had no way of telling. She tried to remember how she used to think when she could eat and sleep. So she said nothing and walked into her apartment, leaving the door open, and lay down on the couch. He followed her and closed the door. From the corner of her eye his shadow moved across the room to a guitar that was propped against the wall.

"Is this yours?" he asked and picked it up, strumming it.

"No. I don't know who it belongs to. One of Marguerite's friends." This was a lie. She could remember the guy's face but little else about him except he'd bought her drinks all night, one right after another like little soldiers in a battalion trying to liberate her mind from its jail.

Jimmy sat on a yellow vinyl kitchen chair by the television and began to tune the guitar, and in a few minutes he was playing something classical, the notes scattering over the dark room like a swarm of fireflies escaping from a jar. Lani felt as if ice were cracking over a hot sea in her chest. She lay on the couch, breathing in the notes that flew from Jimmy Monroe's fingers, the little sparks cascading through her like food and drink, and she remembered him as a skinny boy with a wild thatch of blond curls, quiet, looking down at the ground. When had he learned to do this, make notes careen through this dark room, so real you could almost see them?

After the Bach—it had to be Bach—he started on Bob Dylan. He was playing one of Lani's favorite songs—"Love Minus Zero, No Limit"—from *Bringing It All Back Home*, but his low voice softening out the lyrics like a martini that was equal parts Dylan and Dean Martin, the half-remembered words coming back to her like old friends, until at the end of the song she was that raven with a broken wing. If he'd stopped there, she could have gone back to her job the next day—pitting the cherries for the *clafoutis*, whipping the cream for her famous banana coconut cake, curling the chocolate for her double rum torte—but he kept playing—Tim Buckley's "I Must Have Been Blind," Johnny Cash's "Long Black Veil," Billie Holliday's "God Bless the Child"—until the early sun sneaked in between the slats of the blinds over Marguerite's living room window. By that time her ghosts were in Timbuktu, and she would have gone with Jimmy Monroe to Outer Mongolia just to hear him play "Jesu, Joy of Man's Desiring" before she went to sleep each night, because she finally did sleep—ten hours of deep, dreamless darkness—so that when she woke and he took her out to an all-day breakfast place, she was able to eat two blueberry pancakes, a poached egg, bacon, and drink a glass of milk. Later that day they put the orange couch on the side of the road and piled everything Lani owned into the back of his Chevy pickup. They drove northward singing "I Ain't Gonna Work on Maggie's Farm No More," "Born to Be Wild," "Sisters of Mercy," "I'm in Love, I'm All Shook Up."

When she forgot the lyrics, it was okay, because Jimmy knew them all, just as he could read the map of the knotted highways of California, Oregon, and Washington that looked more like the veins in the arm of a heroin addict than a plan of the highway system that would take them through the small towns and big cities along the Pacific coast.

Jimmy moved through the world as if there were no detours, no dams, no brick walls so thick even a wrecking ball couldn't penetrate them. His world was made of water, and even though the people they met couldn't know about his music, they acted as if they did, because there was music in his voice and in his hands and in his smile. Even waitresses were kind to him, hard-bitten women with plastic nametags that said Edith, Lurleen, Dot, women who had seen their share of dead ends and stop signs if the maps of their faces were telling the truth.

Lani marveled at how he'd find the right motel or campground, how his fingers moved over the guitar strings as he practiced every evening. Sometimes she would dance, barefoot in the motel room, her long feet clean, with trimmed pearly nails, following the rhythm of his song. She loved his voice, the way it moved on the air like some radio broadcast from another world with none of the wild animal screams that came from the regular zoo of zombies that stalked her through the streets of Honolulu and Los Angeles. She hadn't seen her father or Ruby or her *tutu* since Jimmy had picked up that guitar, but she knew they weren't gone. They were following in a Greyhound bus, their screaming scaring the willies out of the migrant workers, teenagers driven away by angry stepfathers, or poor single mothers with black eyes running from the men who would one day kill them.

Lester Higata and the Orchid of Divine Retribution
1975

When the Taniguchis moved to Hawai'i Kai, a *haole* man bought their house on Lipona Street. A young couple helped him move in—his son and daughter-in-law, Katherine Higata guessed, because the two men were carbon copies of each other standing on the sidewalk, the same thin hips and stooped shoulders and thick thatch of wiry hair, black on the younger man, white on the older.

"We have to visit," Katherine said to her husband Lester. They were in his greenhouse in the backyard. It was really more a shed with windows and shelves for the rows of orchids Lester had collected since he and Katherine married over twenty years before. He was repotting a *Paphiopedilum parishii*, loosening the roots from the side of the old pot with a butter knife. The scent in the little room was musty and sweet with the flowering plants, a big showy *Cattleya loddigesii* on the shelf to Lester's right, its butter-yellow petals like an Elizabethan ruff around the cream funnel-shaped lip shot with rosy veins.

Lester nodded, removing the plant from the pot and shaking off the loose potting mixture, his thick fingers searching for discolored or damaged roots and removing them. Turning toward his wife, he smiled and pointed to the larger pot on the shelf near the door. She followed his gaze and handed him the terra cotta container, which he took with his free hand.

"What are we going to do about Paul?" She folded her arms across her chest, her brow knit, her short chestnut curls a little wild in the humidity of the greenhouse. Katherine Higata had turned fifty in January, but she was still as slim as a girl.

"Kathy, he's going to be what he's going to be. He reminds me of my father. He could fix anything. Paul was never good in school. Remember the seven and eight?"

She rolled her eyes. When Paul was in the first grade, she'd worked with him every evening at the kitchen table because he couldn't tell the difference between a seven and an eight. Seven and one—that she could understand—or eight and two, but seven and eight? She'd been spoiled by their daughter Linda, who was two years older. Linda never needed help with her schoolwork. She'd gotten a scholarship to UCLA and was in graduate school there now in psychology while Paul had failed every class he'd taken last semester at Kapi'olani Community College.

"What's he going to do?" she asked.

Lester held the oldest bulb in the clump near the edge of the new pot and filled the cavity below the roots with the loose mix. He loved the blossom of the *Paphiopedilum parishii* with its lime green lip and thin drooping purplish petals like a Fu Manchu mustache.

"He doesn't have to worry about a place to live," Lester said, setting the pot on a high shelf to his right. The slanting roof was made from Plexiglass that let a diffused light into the little shed.

"That was so unfair of your mother to leave Paul the house and Linda nothing." Katherine's blue eyes crackled with resentment.

"Linda doesn't need the house. Who knows if she'll even move back from the mainland when she finishes school. Paul will raise a family there. Linda didn't mind. It's not as if my mother loved Paul more." He turned and put his arms around his wife. His mother had told him once that she was leaving the house to Paul because he looked more Japanese than Linda. What a woman. When she died, a dark shadow lifted off the street, as though a great ugly bird had stretched its wings and flown, leaving behind a few of its feathers.

"That house is the reason he's not trying in school." Katherine pressed her head against her husband's chest.

Lester stepped back and lifted her face. He had been married to her for twenty five years, and still he couldn't believe his luck. "The only reason he got through high school is that you worked with him. He never would have graduated without you."

He looked into her eyes. They wanted to say he was wrong, but she knew he was right. Paul could repair any engine, small or large, automobile or lawn mower, but he couldn't sit still in class. He'd built his own boat that he sailed out from O'ahu every weekend. He'd built Lester's greenhouse when he was only fourteen.

"He'll be fine. He's just not going to be a college graduate." Lester kissed her and held her to his chest again. She sighed and pulled away.

"I know, but I worked so hard with him," she said, her eyes damp now.

"Think about how much Spanish you learned," Lester said, ducking the flat of her palm as it hit his arm. "Buenos dias, Señora Higata," he laughed. She was laughing now, too. When they went to Oaxaca for a vacation, she'd known more Spanish than Paul.

"How about if I take him that *Cattleya*," Lester said, looking at one of his least favorite blooms—a ruffled lavender with a darker purple lip, what most people thought of as an orchid, that and the little purple flowers that were grown to make leis.

"What would Paul do with an orchid?"

"Not Paul, our new neighbor." Lester took down the pot and brushed off the sides. He preferred the darker blooms, the spiky *Laeliocattleya*'s red cluster of flowers or the *Laelia harpophylla*, like a flock of coral birds.

"Are you going to ask him to go to church?" Katherine brushed the front of her blouse where Lester had left some potting mix.

"Sure, but he may already have one."

"I'll make some cookies."

He nodded and walked back to the house with her, holding the bloom of the lavender *Cattleya* away from him so he wouldn't bruise it.

After dinner they walked across the street, Lester holding the orchid and Katherine with a plate of chocolate chip cookies covered with foil. Although it was August, a strong trade wind was coming off the ocean and cooling the street, ruffling the fronds of the palm trees and shaking the mangoes on Mr. Manago's trees.

Lester knocked on the door. A chair scraped along the floor in the back of the house and footsteps echoed on wood floors.

The man with gray hair answered the door. He was short with a little barrel of a chest.

"I'm Katherine Higata from across the street, and this is my husband, Lester. We wanted to welcome you to Lipona Street. I made these cookies. I hope you like chocolate chip."

The man took the plate and stepped aside. "Please, come in. My name is Alfred Friedmann. Thank you. I like chocolate chip very much." His accent was soft, and his English very elegant and clipped.

Katherine and Lester slipped off their shoes and entered Mr. Friedmann's darkened living room. He put the plate of cookies on a table by the door, and flipped the switch on a lamp, which lent its dull glow to the room.

"Please, sit down. I've just made a pot of coffee. I'll bring some out, shall I?" He paused as though he were on the verge of bowing but then smiled and turned and went down the hall, returning in a few minutes carrying a silver tray with a china coffeepot and three delicate matching china cups and saucers. He set the tray down on the coffee table and turned to Katherine. "Would you like to pour?"

He placed Katherine's plate of cookies on the table, her cheap plastic plate next to the elegant silver tray. She passed the cookies to him and he took one and looked at the top, the chocolate pieces poking out of the dark tan cookie, and then turned it over and inspected the flat bottom.

"Very good," he said after biting into it.

They learned that he had just moved to Hawai'i from New York. He'd taught biology at Columbia, but when his wife died, the winters were too cold, even with the opera and art galleries. His son taught at UH, and on visits he found he loved the weather. He sold his apartment in New York and bought this little house on Lipona Street because it was near the university, and he could walk to the stores and take the bus. His son and wife lived in Mānoa with their two small children.

"I never would have predicted such a place for myself as a boy growing up in Budapest," he said finishing his coffee. "Now all I need is a small car so I can drive to Ala Moana each morning to swim in the ocean."

When the Higatas rose to leave, Mr. Friedmann walked ahead of them to the door. Katherine poked Lester, who shook his head and told his new neighbor to let the *Cattleya* dry out before watering it.

As they were crossing the street, Katherine said, "Why didn't you invite him to church?"

"He's Jewish."

"So, what? They're God's chosen people. There's a place for him in our church." She looked back at the man on the porch, but he had gone inside and closed his door. Sometimes Katherine's fervor surprised Lester. He had been content as a Buddhist, and now as a Christian he felt much the same.

"I had a feeling it was too soon to ask him," Lester said, closing the door of their house and locking it for the night.

Two days later Mr. Friedmann brought Katherine's plate back to her. She was at a Women's Missionary Union meeting, but Lester was home and ended up showing his neighbor his greenhouse.

"This is a sound structure." Alfred Friedmann walked around the little building constructed of glass windows and doors in a wooden frame. Paul had stained it dark green to blend in with the foliage of the backyard garden, the torch ginger and plumeria trees that hid their house from those surrounding them.

"My son built it from materials we found." Lester turned on the light and the orchids were illuminated like another set of lights. A *Phalaenopsis mariae* was blooming, a long stem of magenta and white flowers fluttering in the glare of the bulb.

"This is a *Cattleya dowiana*." Lester showed him a plant he'd just bought that day. "When it blooms, Mr. Friedmann, it will have a large orange lip and bright yellow petals."

"Please call me Alfred," he said, contemplating the fleshy green leaves of the orchid. "I find myself a city man in the midst of a city, but it's one that is also a garden."

"Not for very much longer, I'm afraid," said Lester. "We had a chance to keep the old Honolulu, but we said no."

"I'm afraid I don't understand."

"That highway two blocks away. Fifteen years ago we could have planned for a rail system. We would have been a city of the future. Instead we chose to become a little Los Angeles."

"Is it too late?"

"It's never too late," said Lester. "But the main objection was money, and it won't be any less expensive next year." He turned off the lights in the greenhouse and offered Alfred a glass of iced tea. They sat on the metal chairs on the brick patio he and Paul had laid down last summer. This was Lester's favorite time of day, when the light was almost lavender. The roar of H1 was like an ocean in the distance.

"Where is your wife this evening?" Mr. Friedmann sipped his tea and set the glass on the table between them.

"At a meeting at church. I may as well ask you, because she is going to if I don't. We attend a Baptist church. If you'd care to join us, you would be very welcome."

"I'm Jewish," he said. "However, I haven't been to synagogue since my mother died. I am a man of science."

"Are science and religion incompatible?"

"For me, they are. For a Jewish man my age from Europe, it is either impossible or essential to believe in God."

"I understand," Lester said, breathing in the sweet evening air. His plumerias were scenting the yard.

"I lost my entire family in the camps, my father, brothers, my wife and two boys, everyone except for my mother. I was nearly killed by the Nazis. Europe during the war is impossible to imagine now, especially in this beautiful place." He let his arms rest on the tops of his thighs, the pale skin shimmering in the fading light.

"I was in Europe during the war," Lester said after a long silence. "After Pearl Harbor a lot of Japanese boys volunteered for the army. We looked like the enemy, but we were Americans. I was part of the liberation of Dachau. I try not to think about what I saw. At church the minister talks about hell. I've seen hell."

"And you can still believe in God?"

"It was hard after the war, not just Dachau but seeing my friends killed. I saw one boy's head blown off his neck. He was as close as you are to me now. I thought I'd never clean his blood off my face. But I fell in love with my wife and she believes, so I decided to believe. Especially with children. You want them to believe in a better world."

"I suppose. My son is a scientist, but he attends the synagogue for his children, too. Yahweh is entirely capable of the world of the camps, but your Christ? This is not his world. The messiah is for dreamers."

Lester looked up at the sky, deep blue but with the shadows of clouds still moving as if being chased by one of those old Hawaiian gods. It was funny how people came up with the gods they needed. Jesus was a lot of things, but he wasn't a weather god, but then neither was the Buddha.

"I was raised a Buddhist," he said to Mr. Freidmann. "Is it the Buddha's world?"

"Not for Jews. For Jews it's a world that Yahweh built—cruel, harsh, always winter, even in June, even when the sun is shining and the birds are singing, and your thoughts are turning to love, because what is love but hormones calling to one another and if you're lucky they are the hormones that you can live with for twenty or thirty years, long enough to raise another generation. Turn the other cheek—I ask you. We were acting like Christians, and what did that get us?"

Lester thought about the day they drove toward Dachau, and he saw the emaciated people wandering around in filthy black-

and-white rags. It was April, but clumps of snow were still on the ground. Hundreds of people were stumbling over the fields. They were almost skeletons with a thin layer of flesh stretched over the bones. At first the soldiers didn't know what to think, but a few of the prisoners spoke English. They told them they had worked in factories during the war.

"I sometimes see things that make me believe in God," he said finally, speaking more to the evening than to Mr. Friedmann, who shrugged.

A light went on in the kitchen. It was too early for Katherine, so when Paul walked down the back steps into the yard, Lester wasn't surprised. He introduced his son to Mr. Friedmann.

"Where's Mom?" Paul asked, sitting down on another chair. He was carrying a bottle of beer.

"Church."

"What a surprise," said Paul, finishing his beer and setting the bottle on the uneven bricks of the patio. Later Lester would put the bottle in the trash so Katherine wouldn't see it.

Paul stretched his lanky frame out. He did look more Japanese than his sister, but you could see the *haole* in him, too, his hair dark brown rather than black and his eyes wider than Lester's. All the days he'd spent at the beach and on his boat had turned his skin a cocoa color with a tint of pink on his cheeks.

"I sailed to Kaua'i today," Paul said. "I met a guy who has sailed with his grandfather past Ni'ihau to the western islands. I'd like to do that. Maybe this summer you and I could go."

Lester nodded. "How long do you think it would take?"

"Maybe two, three weeks. What do you think Mom would say?"

"We'd have to get her used to the idea. She won't like it at first, but she'll be okay with it once she's thought about it a while."

Paul sat up. "Do you know anyone who needs a car? My friend Mark has a great little Ford for sale. His grandmother died, and she only had it for two years."

"Why doesn't he want to keep it?"

"He has a new Camaro. It's a sweet little car for someone. A great deal."

Mr. Friedmann cleared his throat. "I'm looking for a car."

Paul turned to him. "Do you want to drive out tomorrow and see it?"

Mr. Friedmann bent his head to the side and forward. "How much is he asking for it?"

"Two thousand. That's really a steal."

"It is a good price. I was looking in the newspaper, and everything was much more. Where does your friend live?"

"In Wai'anae, near Mākaha."

Lester glanced at Mr. Friedmann. How did he explain Wai'anae? "It's a little town about an hour away, maybe more," said Lester. Wai'anae was a dusty little town at the end of Farrington Highway, known for its gangs and drug problems. When Lester was a boy his father had taken him to Wai'anae many times to see his friend Mr. Agena, who had a farm down Lualualei Homestead Road. They would go out on Mr. Agena's boat and fish off the Leeward coast of O'ahu. Now Lester had his own friend, John Sanford, who had a little mission near where Mr. Agena's farm had been with Mount Ka'ala soaring up from the fertile plains like a temple to the old gods. The old Hawaiians had raised taro in the shadow of the mountain. Mr. Manago, who lived down the street, had grown up in Wai'anae. His brother still owned a dairy farm near John Sanford's mission. Every spring he went to pick up a truckload of manure for the mango trees he grew in the lot between his house and Helen Nakamura's.

The next day was Saturday, and they started before the sun got really hot. Wai'anae was on the leeward side of the island, sheltered from the rains off the ocean by the jutting mountains that divided the island. Farrington Highway was an old two-lane highway that circled Pearl Harbor and went inland past Waipahu and 'Ewa Beach and then hugged the shore along the west side of the island through the little towns of Nānākuli and Mā'ili. This was a part of the island that the tourists didn't see, the mangy dogs searching around trash cans, kids with nothing to do but body surf or play tetherball in the swept dirt front yards that clustered around the highway.

The traffic wasn't too bad, so they arrived about nine o'clock. Paul's friend Mark was working on the Ford in the carport of his house, a little wooden structure with a curving Japanese roof, painted pink with green eaves.

"Hey, brah," Mark said to Paul and clasped his hand in an intricate handshake. Mark was a dark, broad-shouldered boy with a wide chest that tapered down to his blue-and-white flowered baggies.

"This is my father, Lester," Paul said to Mark, "and his friend Mr. Friedmann." Mark wiped his hands on a greasy cloth and shook the two older men's hands.

"This is the car," he said pointing to the Ford, its white paint gleaming in the soft morning sun. "My *tutu* only had it two years. It has 15,000 miles on it. The only reason for that is my sister lives in Kailua, and the old lady would drive over there every week to see the kids."

Lester and Mr. Friedmann walked around the car, looking for dings, but the body was smooth and the chrome shined.

"When Paul called and said you were coming I waxed her up. She looks pretty good, yeah?" Mark wiped the silver metal near the driver's window with a clean cloth.

Paul ran his hand over the hood of the car. His hands were large, and the nails were so bitten that the tops of his fingers were clubbed. Figuring out the difference between that seven and eight had been really tough on Paul, thought Lester, though seeing his hands against the white metal reminded him of his father's hands painting their house in Waialua white, his large hands gripping the paintbrush and the rounded tips of his bitten fingers.

For Lester watching his son was like seeing his father alive again. Paul was taller and had his mother's *haole* blood, but Paul moved like Lester's father, like an ocelot or jaguar they sometimes saw on television nature shows, moving through the jungle as if he were a part of it as much as the trees and vines and the earth itself. It was a miracle that he had finished school. Poor Katherine, she had tried so hard, but keeping this boy inside was not going to work. He was made to put things together and take them apart—radios, houses, boats, cars. Even as a little boy, they had to beg him to come in at night. He would hide under the house, crouching behind a post until Lester brought out his flashlight and caught the shape of a little boy in the darkness.

"Why don't you two take the car out and test it," Mark said. "I'll keep Paul here as hostage." He handed Mr. Friedmann the keys.

Lester got into the passenger's side of the car, the faint smell of stale tobacco smoke curled around him like a glove. Although he'd quit ten years before, he never lost his longing for a cigarette, the sweet poison of the smoke snaking down his throat and into his lungs. Like a lot of GIs, he had learned to smoke in the war, the two-pack of Luckies a little miracle you found at the bottom of your K rations.

"Where shall we go?" Mr. Friedmann asked as he backed out of the driveway.

Lester watched his son talking to Mark, who was laughing at something Paul had said, maybe some joke about what a fuddy-duddy his father was. When he had been nineteen, he had thought that life was going in a certain way, and then Pearl Harbor. Nothing was ever the same.

Mr. Friedmann cleared his throat. They were at Farrington Highway.

"Take a right," Lester said, "I have a friend who lives just outside town. Let's drive to his place."

They took a right on Lualualei Homestead Road and in a few minutes were in the country. Old Quonset huts from World War II were nestled in the deep shade of monkeypods and banana trees. Chickens pecked along the road, kicking up gravel with their claws and looking around in alarm as the car rolled by.

"Who is your friend?" asked Mr. Friedmann after they'd driven for a few minutes.

"John Sanford. He's the minister of a mission out here that the Wai'anae church sponsored. His wife and children came out here with him, but she moved to Honolulu with most of the children. His oldest son was killed in Vietnam. I think another one of his boys lives out here with him now."

On a deep shady part of the road, this seemed like another world. Lester sometimes thought if there were bubbles in time, this would be the place where suddenly warriors would erupt from the jungle or ancient Hawaiians would walk from their taro fields. On the right, they passed a mango grove, the trees soft and arching, studded with their gold and mauve fruit. Maybe this was where Mr. Manago, his neighbor across the street in Honolulu, had gotten the idea for his mango trees. The dairy farm he'd grown up on wasn't far from here.

They took another right but passed right by the mission and had to turn around at a crossroad. Lester had forgotten about the houses around the mission. They pulled up in front of two Quonset huts. One was the parsonage and the other the church. Outside was a black-and-white sign on plywood: Ka'ala View Mission.

John Sanford was clipping the hibiscus bush on one side of the church door. The red flowers danced in the breeze from the ocean, framed by the dark green of the Quonset hut. When he saw Lester, he waved and walked over to the car. He was a tall man, maybe six-five, and thin.

"Brother Higata. What a surprise! No one comes out to visit us." He wiped his balding forehead with his handkerchief, rubbed his hands, and then shook Lester's hand.

"This is my new neighbor, Mr. Friedmann. We're test driving this car. I thought we'd stop by and say hello."

"I'm so glad you did. It was getting too hot for this. Why don't we sit on the lanai and have something cold to drink? I think we have some iced tea."

He led them to the other Quonset hut, which had a screened porch attached to the side facing the church. Lester and Mr. Friedmann sat on the cushioned bamboo couch, and John Sanford brought in a pitcher of ice water.

"Sorry, I guess my son drank the last of the tea before he left for the beach." Setting the tray on a bamboo coffee table, he poured three glasses of ice water and then sat down on a cushioned chair that matched the couch.

"John and I were in Italy at the same time, different battalions but same war," Lester said to Alfred Friedmann.

"I was a part of the assault on Sicily," John Sanford said. "They said that Lucky Luciano worked with the army and the Mafia in Sicily. We encountered so little resistance, at the time. If I had believed in God, I would have said He was keeping us safe."

"But it was the Mafia?" Mr. Friedmann said.

"That's what they say. The Lord works in mysterious ways his miracles to declare. Are you a churchgoing man, Mr. Friedmann?"

"I'm afraid not. The Lord's ways are too mysterious for me."

"The war seems so far away in this place. Is that a *Loddigesii* I see by that ginger?" Lester stood and pointed to an orchid blooming in a table of terra cotta pots to the side of the lanai. John Sanford turned his gaze to the splotch of gold ten feet away.

"I don't know, Lester," he said. "Those are Caroline's plants. I don't suppose she'll ever come and get them now." His eyes were vacant as if he were watching a movie of his wife tending her orchids, a grainy movie that was fading as he watched.

"It's beautiful," Lester said, motioning to Mr. Friedmann to follow him. "Let me show you the petals. Sometimes you can see a network of cream-colored veins."

They escaped the lanai for the stand of ginger, the red blooms like splashes of blood against the green leaves. Mr. Sanford followed them, but he was slumped over a bit.

"Why don't you take it with you," he said to Lester.

"Oh, no," said Lester. "I couldn't take Caroline's orchid."

"Caroline doesn't want it, and if she does you'll take better care of it than I do. Take them all. I'll get some newspapers."

The three men loaded the orchids into the back of Mark's dead grandmother's car. The trunk was empty except for a Barbie doll in a black-and-white swimsuit and black high-heeled shoes. Barbie's blonde ponytail was a little dirty, but otherwise she looked ready for a day at the beach. Lester placed each pot on the newspapers, but the blooming plant he laid on its side and stuffed paper against the soil, so it wouldn't fall out as they drove.

"Tell Caroline she can have these anytime she wants." Lester shook Sanford's hand, and they drove off. Lester looked back, and his friend was standing, shoulders stooped in front of the green Quonset hut, Mount Ka'ala jutting up in the distance like the body of a giant god ready to lurch up and crush the world under his feet. Divine retribution was something Lester and Katherine discussed often. If God loved us so much, why was He so cruel? Katherine was a die-hard Calvinist—God gave people a choice. But Lester wasn't satisfied. Why had he made us so stupid? The world was beautiful. Even outside Dachau, the sky had been blue as the last snows of winter melted in the afternoon sun. Grass was coming up under the clumps of snow, and little wildflowers would soon follow—buttercups, daisies, Queen Anne's lace, sunflowers.

And if people weren't stupid, they were crazy or sick or maimed. Sometimes it was hard to believe that God was even interested in his creation. For Lester, it was easier to believe in Jesus, a good man who had tried to show others how to live. But what about a man like Sanford, who had given up everything to do the Lord's work?

When they turned by the mango grove, Lester said, "I shouldn't have taken his wife's orchids."

"He's right," Mr. Friedmann said, staring straight ahead. "You'll take better care of them than he has."

Lester nodded, but his stomach felt queasy, like the rolling stormy ocean right off the coast. The orchids had still been blooming, and in the dry Wai'anae weather they would have continued to bloom.

"Do you like the car?" he said to stop thinking about the orchids in the trunk of the car, their roots cramped in the old pots.

"Yes," Alfred said. "It's an excellent car, just what I was looking for."

"Good." Lester swallowed hard and thought of Sanford standing in front of his empty mission as they drove away, his wife's orchids now in the trunk of a car that had belonged to another woman, one who spent her last days driving from Wai'anae to Kailua, down Farrington Highway, past Mā'ili and Nānākuli and then the fancy beach houses where a big television star was said to live, past the power plant with its giant smoking towers, past Waipahu and 'Aiea and over the Pali to see her grandchildren, her blood flowing in the veins of other beings, something as mysterious as it was easy to explain.

And John Sanford, standing in front of the two Quonset huts, watched Lester and Mr. Friedmann drive away as he had watched his wife leave for the new house she'd bought in Honolulu with the money her father left her when he died. His boy, Johnny, had been at his side then, but Johnny was dead now, buried in Punchbowl with the men who'd fought with him and Lester in Italy and through France into Germany. It was in Italy that he'd become friends with Morris Kimbrell, a chaplain. Morris had brought him to Jesus and to the college in Virginia where he met Caroline. They had been so young, and she had been so beautiful. How could he have thought a woman like that could live in such a place? But for years she had worked beside him, had eight children. Then one day she locked him out of their bedroom. How had he lost her? She said she couldn't have another child, and yet she loved them all. He tried to explain that it was God's way of populating heaven, but she said she would kill herself if she got pregnant again.

When Sanford first came to O'ahu twelve years before, he thought how like Sicily it was, a volcanic island in the middle of the blue sea, and though the people here spoke his language, he could never understand their ways. They were as mysterious to him as the squat Italian peasant men plowing fields with mules and harnesses. How could he bring God's word to them, when he couldn't eat what they ate, sleep as they slept, move as they moved through their days? It was as though there was a light shining on their world, beyond the sun, beyond the moon and stars, shimmering in the leaves and flowers and fruit. Lester Higata had seen it in Caroline's orchids. Why had he let Lester take them? Now he had nothing of her left, nothing but the photograph on his desk, but it was so small and blurry the woman could have been almost anyone at all.

Sayonara,
Mrs. Higata
1969

Katherine Higata placed a glass of water between her mother-in-law's dry lips and tilted the glass so the water moistened her mouth. Mrs. Higata had breast cancer, and Katherine had moved into her house for what the doctor said were her final weeks.

"Gloria's here," Katherine said to Mrs. Higata. "I'll be back around ten."

The older woman turned her head to the wall and waved her hand toward the door.

In the kitchen Gloria, Katherine's sister-in-law, said, "Mom was always so nasty to you. I can't believe you're doing this."

"Oh, she wasn't so bad." But even as she said it Katherine felt how hard it was sometimes to take the comments that slid out of Mrs. Higata's mouth like snakes. She pretended as if she didn't understand, but Mrs. Higata knew she did.

"She's my mother, and I can barely stand coming over here every other day," Gloria said, lighting a cigarette. Gloria's skirt was so short Katherine couldn't believe they let her teach at Roosevelt High. Katherine and Gloria were the same age, but Gloria dressed like Katherine's sixteen-year-old daughter Linda.

"Gloria," Katherine said, "you can't smoke around her."

"I know. I know. I don't smoke in the room. Anyway, she's dying."

"I want to make her as comfortable as possible," Katherine said, checking the back door to make sure it was locked.

Gloria shrugged. She came over every other evening, so Katherine could go home and have dinner with Lester and their two children at their house on the next block of Lipona Street. On the other nights, Mrs. Niitani from next door would come over and sit with Mrs. Higata until Katherine returned around ten o'clock.

Lester was cooking and shopping, but Katherine wanted to eat with them and talk to Linda and Paul before they went to sleep. Linda was a junior in high school, and Katherine was alarmed by how beautiful her daughter had become. For the past two years boys had been swarming around like flies. She'd seen it happen the summer Linda turned fifteen. Before that she'd been shaped like a hot dog, but during the summer of 1967, she had acquired a waist, and nothing was the same. Linda was mystified by her own power. A policeman asked her on a date when he stopped her for making an illegal turn. "Do I have to go out with him?" she asked Katherine. "He didn't give me a ticket."

The week before, Linda and Katherine had fought over a bathing suit in the Daisy Chain, a little boutique near Liberty House at Ala Moana. Linda tried on a white piqué bikini that was so small it scared Katherine. She knew she wouldn't be able to send Linda out in a two-piece, but this was out of the question. After muffled words through clenched teeth, they compromised on a blue-and-white gingham bikini that had at least three more inches of fabric than the white suit.

Paul was a different matter. He was fourteen and small for his age, and he only had one friend, Stuart Wurst, who was six-two and had a thatch of wild blond kinky hair. All they did was buy comic books and talk about who was more powerful, Green Lantern or Batman. She had to be home to make sure Paul did his homework. He didn't care if he failed. This was as mysterious to Katherine as Linda's waist.

Mrs. Higata didn't need much. Katherine sat with her until she went to sleep, and then she stretched out on the other single bed in the room. She was a light sleeper, so any sound the older woman made would wake her. Katherine loved the nighttime. The sounds of the city in the distance and the sweet smell of the night air reminded her of her nursing days after the war when she was on the night shift at the old Tripler Hospital. The wards were quiet, the wounded men sleeping, and she'd sit and listen to the trade winds ruffling the palms and think about the world she'd left on the mainland. During those nights, she'd decided to stay in Hawai'i. She loved everything about the islands—the green of the mountains and the blue of the skies, but especially the nights, so cool and fragrant after a rain, the red earth sharp and the plumerias sweet as they were now, their scent floating through the windows of her mother-in-law's bedroom.

When Katherine returned after dinner, she said goodbye to Gloria and locked the front door behind her. Mrs. Higata was sleeping, but she'd wake soon. She never slept for more than an hour or two and woke thirsty. Her face was dry and the skin taut over the bones of her skull. Gloria was right. Mrs. Higata had always been nasty to everyone except Katherine and Lester's son Paul. Katherine and Lester speculated on what drew her to her grandson. He never tried to please her, but she liked everything he did. She liked it that he looked more Japanese than Linda, but Lester and Gloria were as Japanese as Mrs. Higata, and she treated them the same as she did Katherine.

At two o'clock Katherine woke to the older woman moving in her bed, the sheets rustling as if a moth were trapped where Mrs. Higata's left hand was. Katherine sat up and put her bare feet on the floor. She thought of the slippers she used to wear during the cold winters in Ohio where she'd lived as a girl. No one in Ohio went barefoot except kids in July and August, but in

Hawai'i, no one wore shoes in the house. They slipped them off before walking through the door. There was a little shelf on their front porches or right inside the door for shoes and slippers.

Her mother-in-law's hand escaped from under the sheet and clawed at the air.

"Where's the light?" she said. "I can't see in the dark."

Katherine switched on the lamp between their beds. The dim bulb threw a soft light on the powdery skin of Mrs. Higata. Katherine thought how odd it was that she still addressed her as "Mrs. Higata" after twenty years. For the first few months she was married, when people called Katherine Mrs. Higata, she had flinched. She never realized that her married name would be the same as this woman's though, of course, she knew she'd take Lester's name.

She picked up Mrs. Higata's wrist and found her pulse, light and fast, and looked at her watch.

"Am I still alive?" Mrs. Higata asked.

Katherine smiled and wrote down the pulse in her notebook. "You're still here," she said, "alive and kicking."

"Hah," spat Mrs. Higata. "Not kicking so much anymore. Where are Lester and Gloria? They're my children. They should be here."

"Don't you remember? Lester came by after work, and Gloria sat with you while I went home for dinner."

"I remember. I'm dying, not stupid. They should be here."

"Lester has to work in the morning. Gloria, too. Anyway I'm a nurse. I know what to do, and I could take off at my job. I have a lot of leave saved." Katherine pulled down the sheets and exposed the frail body of her mother-in-law, her nightgown bunched up around her waist, and her white underpants baggy around the concave of her abdomen.

"Do you want to get up and go to the bathroom?"

Mrs. Higata didn't answer, but she lifted herself up with Katherine's help and let her half-lead, half-carry her to the bathroom.

"Leave me alone and close the door," Mrs. Higata said, her voice raspy. Her once neatly styled hair now looked like the wig of a Kabuki actor, wild and with an inch of gray showing between her scalp and the jet-black dye.

Katherine did as she was told but stood by the closed door, so she could hear if Mrs. Higata needed her.

In a few minutes she called out, and Katherine opened the door and brought her back to the bed. Mrs. Higata lay back, and Katherine pulled the sheets over her.

"It's cold in here," she said. "Why don't you shut that window?"

"Let me pull the blanket up," Katherine said. "If I close the window, it'll get stuffy in here, and you won't like that."

Mrs. Higata opened her mouth to speak then pursed her lips shut.

Why don't you just say it? Katherine thought. You've never been nice before. Why start now when you're dying? Then she looked at the withered face of the woman in the bed. This was her husband's mother. Would Paul's wife feel the same way about her?

"Water," Mrs. Higata whispered.

Katherine turned to pour some water, but the pitcher was empty. That Gloria—she could never be trusted to do anything.

"I'm going to the kitchen to get some more water," Katherine said and straightened the blanket. "I'll be right back."

Mrs. Higata shook her head back and forth, but her eyes were closed. Katherine walked down the hall. The house was like a creature itself, quiet and sleeping. Mrs. Higata's furniture was all from Japan. She'd bought it when she bought the house after the war with the money from her husband's life insurance. The living room was glowing, the street light through the picture window reflected in the plastic covers Mrs. Higata had put on all the furniture, the reds and blues muted as if under a glossy lake.

The rooms were so bright Katherine didn't have to turn on the lights. As she filled the pitcher, she looked out into Mrs. Higata's backyard. The bushes were trimmed in sharp angles, the hibiscus blooms peeping out of the walls of green as if they were pink and red birds in a cage. The light was on in the house next door, and she could see Mrs. Niitani walking around behind the thin curtains in her kitchen. Katherine looked at the wall clock above the stove. It was two-thirty. What in the world was she doing at this time of night? Katherine turned off the water and checked the back door to make sure it was locked. With all the drugs coming from Vietnam, it wasn't safe anymore. Just last week Mr. and Mrs. Manago down the street had their television stolen.

Back in the bedroom, Mrs. Higata was still shaking her head, but now she was murmuring as well. Katherine put the pitcher down and sat in the chair by the bed. Mrs. Higata's pulse was fast.

"Minoru, Minoru," she said, her lips hardly moving. This was her husband's name. He'd been dead for twenty-five years. "Minoru," she said again and let out a low moan. She sounded like an animal, a dog or cat that had been run over by a car but wasn't quite gone. Then she said something else, a string of disjointed words.

"What?" Katherine said, but her mother-in-law was speaking Japanese.

Again she let out a string of staccato words like the rapid fire of a drumbeat.

"What is it?" Katherine said. "Please speak English."

Mrs. Higata's head was thrashing back and forth now as if a strong wind were blowing through the window, a storm from the ocean. Then suddenly her eyes opened wide, and she grabbed Katherine's wrist like one of those monsters in the horror movies Paul loved to watch on television late at night. Her grip was tight and her whole body rigid. Again she said something in Japanese, this time more urgent.

Katherine didn't know what to do. She didn't want to wake Lester. He had a big meeting the next day, and he needed his rest, but what if Mrs. Higata was trying to say something important? People often did at the end of their lives. She remembered all the boys who had died in the hospital after the war. She'd heard the most terrible things sitting by their beds late at night, things they'd done as children, but mostly what they had seen in the war, the heads blown apart, friends killed right in front of them. Why me? they'd ask over and over. Why me? Or they'd tell her who they loved, who would miss them when they were gone.

Then she thought of little Mrs. Niitani next door, puttering around, not sleeping. She ran to the phone and called her number. Mrs. Higata was still rocking and talking.

The phone rang seven times before Mrs. Niitani picked up.

"Hello." Her voice sounded far away, as though she were in Japan.

"Mrs. Niitani, this is Katherine Higata next door. I saw your light. I didn't know who else to call. Lester is asleep. Mrs. Higata is upset, and she's speaking Japanese. It might be important. Can you come over?"

Katherine could hear her breathing.

"Mrs. Niitani? Are you there?"

"Oh, yes. I come right away."

The phone clicked down hard. Back in the bedroom Mrs. Higata was still talking, faster now. Katherine knew enough Japanese that she could tell the older woman was repeating herself.

In a few minutes Katherine heard a little knock on the front door. Mrs. Niitani wore a faded blue muumuu and black rubber slippers on her feet. She followed Katherine back to the bedroom and sat down in the chair beside the bed. Mrs. Higata's head was moving back and forth, and a deep frown knit her brows. "Minoru," she said. "Minoru," and then two or three quick Japanese phrases.

"Can you understand what she's saying?" asked Katherine, who was sitting on the other bed, her hands folded on her lap.

"I understand," said Mrs. Niitani, nodding her head in rhythm to Mrs. Higata, who was still talking, her eyes wide open.

"What's she saying?" Katherine asked.

"Just a minute," Mrs. Niitani said, taking one of Mrs. Higata's hands and leaning closer. She said something in Japanese, and Mrs. Higata replied with a quick, sharp phrase. Mrs. Niitani said something else, but Mrs. Higata stopped talking as suddenly as she had started, looking as if she were a balloon that was losing its air, deflating on the pillow.

Katherine felt the air in the room quiet down when Mrs. Higata stopped talking. After a few minutes her breathing calmed down and became even.

"I think she's asleep," Katherine said to Mrs. Niitani, who sat with her plump hands on her stomach.

Mrs. Niitani said nothing.

"What did she say?" asked Katherine.

Mrs. Niitani shook her head and closed her mouth, her soft little face all at once hard as a piece of lava rock.

"What is it?" asked Katherine.

"It's bad. She didn't know she was telling anyone," Mrs. Niitani said.

Katherine almost didn't want to hear what Mrs. Higata had said. What if it was something terrible about Lester? She didn't want to know. What if it would hurt Lester? Katherine sat on the bed, the figure of Mrs. Higata under her white blanket a mountain between her and Mrs. Niitani, who sat still as a cat.

"She wasn't talking to us," Mrs. Niitani finally said. "She thought she was talking to her husband."

"Minoru," said Katherine.

"Minoru," Mrs. Niitani said. "She said she was sorry she put poison in his musubi. She was mad because he had a girlfriend. She afraid he going divorce her. She say she buy this house with insurance money. It his house, so she going leave it to Paul, because he so much like."

Mrs. Niitani's words vibrated in the room as if they had come from a giant timpani or cymbals. At first the words were so strange that Katherine thought Mrs. Niitani might still be speaking Japanese, but at the same time she knew the words were English.

"I thought he drowned," Katherine said.

"She say she give him musubi to take on boat when he go out to fish." Mrs. Niitani had grabbed the loose fabric of her faded muumuu and was kneading it as though she were making bread. "She so angry. She want to make him sick, but maybe he fall in water. When they find the body, they never check for poison."

Katherine sat without moving. Mrs. Niitani's words were now buzzing around in the room like bees escaped from a hive. This was the same room, the same house Katherine had been coming to for almost twenty years, but everything was different, so changed that they might as well be in a different country where everything red was green, and everything green, yellow. She read in the newspaper about young people taking drugs. She worried about Linda when she went to concerts at the HIC and the Waikiki Shell. She knew some of the people at these concerts took drugs. Was this how they felt? It was the same world, but not the same world.

"What should we do?" asked Mrs. Niitani. "Are you going to tell your husband?"

"No," said Katherine, surprising herself. "If you won't say anything, I won't."

The room went quiet, as if all the bees had flown once again into Mrs. Higata's mouth, which was open like a little withered flower. This woman, thought Katherine, she had been young once, too. What was she like as a girl in Japan before she sailed to Hawai'i to be the bride of Minoru Higata? In a black-and-white photograph on the bureau, Katherine saw a young girl in a kimono standing beside her mother and father. Mrs. Higata came from an educated family, but her father died of tuberculosis when Mrs. Higata was a teenager. One time she said she'd come to Hawai'i because she was always hungry. Katherine thought of her own two children, who had never been hungry.

"We pretend we never hear what she say," said Mrs. Niitani.

Katherine nodded.

Mrs. Niitani stood up and pressed her wrinkled muumuu flat with her pudgy hands. "I go home now. I was cleaning refrigerator when you called." She bustled down the hall like a little locomotive.

Katherine heard the door slam, and the house was quiet again. She wished she could clear her mind of Mrs. Higata's words as easily as she could clean her own refrigerator. That the words were in a language she didn't speak, couldn't understand, made it even more mysterious, like the stories she read about Ava Gardner or Lana Turner in the magazines at her friend Miriam's beauty shop. There were so many worlds in the same world. The world of the movie stars was alien to her, but her daughter Linda's world of beach parties and concerts was foreign, too, as was Mrs. Niitani's world of late-night scrubbing, and Mrs. Higata's Japanese world that would end when she took her last breath.

Of all those people Katherine understood Mrs. Niitani best. She knew how to take care of her family—shop at the supermarket, cook chicken and rice, scrub the linoleum of her kitchen floor, press her daughter's dresses, listen to her husband's worries over a blueprint or a meeting. She also knew the world of nursing—how to read a chart, give an injection, make a bed with a patient lying in it, calm a worried mother, father, husband, wife. And there was the church, her pastor, the children in her Sunday School class, the Bible study she and Lester attended on Wednesday evenings.

This was her world, and everyone she met spoke words she understood. In her years in Hawai'i, she'd met people from all over, some who spoke English, some who didn't. An older Filipino man with lung cancer had made her understand with gestures that he wanted to marry her. When Katherine laughed and pointed to her wedding ring, he placed his hands over his heart and looked as if it were broken. Katherine had seen a healthy woman die two weeks after her husband of fifty years dropped dead with a stroke. She had tended the knife wounds of a sobbing man who had just killed his brother. She had listened to the hallucinations of men who would never be able to come home from war. No, she hadn't heard Mrs. Higata, for the other woman had spoken in a language Katherine didn't understand, a language from a country Katherine had seen but would never go to as long as she lived.

The
Thirty
Names
of Kū
1962

Ruby Kaapuni was having her first mai tai of the evening at Kono's, a little bar on the Ala Wai side of Kalākaua in Waikīkī. Gilbert Kono himself was behind the bar, a big man in a green aloha shirt with red hibiscus flowers exploding across its surface like kisses or little fires. Ruby was talking to Richard Carstens from Bloomington, Indiana. She'd liked him right away—his short brush of blond hair with its pale scalp underneath, the blue eyes behind wire-rimmed glasses, the white drip-dry shirt tucked into his black slacks. After her first drink, Ruby tried to imagine the feet in his black loafers, narrow and bony with big toes curved inward, the yellowing toenails a little too long, feet that hadn't seen the sun since summer, like some soft fish that swam in the cool of the deep ocean. Her own feet were brown and slim, her legs, too, even after two children.

"We have no business there," Richard Carstens was saying, his face pink from sunburn. He was in Honolulu for a conference about the war building up in Southeast Asia. "Everybody in Washington knows it, but they still have that World War II mentality. If we can beat Hitler, we can beat anyone. But Ho Chi Minh is not Hitler. It's 1962 not 1942. This is a civil war. It's going to be a bloodbath."

He signaled to Gilbert, who brought them both fresh drinks. Richard Carstens was drinking bourbon on the rocks, but Ruby Kaapuni was partial to mai tais. There was nothing about a mai tai that Ruby didn't like—the bright parasol, the sweet tartness of the pineapple, and the rum hitting the top of her spinal cord like a sledgehammer, in an instant straightening out even the most jangled and crooked thoughts, smoothing them like sanding a fender crumpled after a six-car pileup on the Pali Highway.

Ruby nodded and thought about Southeast Asia, but she'd never been farther away from Honolulu than the Big Island though her husband went to Japan on business all the time. Two weeks ago she'd been looking in his wallet for a twenty to buy groceries when she came across a photo of a young Japanese girl holding a baby. When she saw the photo, she took everything he had—five hundred dollars—dropped the kids at her mother's house and gave her a hundred for food. She left them watching *The Guiding Light* and eating Cheerios.

Richard Carstens was sad. Ruby liked that in a man. It meant he was thinking about his own problems and not dreaming up trouble for her. When he looked at her, she might as well have been a ghost.

"I'm married," he said, jiggling the ice in his drink and staring down at the cheap laminated wood of the bar.

Of course, he was. Any fool could see his wedding ring, and he looked married, like a tree that wasn't a sapling anymore, one with roots that could stay in the ground even when winds were screaming off the ocean.

"Me, too," Ruby said. "I have two kids—Chris and Lani. 'Lani' means 'heaven' in Hawaiian. I wanted her to have a big name to help her move through the world."

He looked at her and then back at his drink. "What are you doing here?"

She shook her head. It was a complicated question, like drawing a map of the route her ancestors had taken over the Pacific from Tahiti. Everything that had happened to her had led her to Kono's, and if she were lucky, she'd move on tomorrow the way a wave moves through the ocean, carrying fish, seaweed, and boats along with it.

"I should be out with other people at the conference," he said to the bar or maybe to his drink, "but they make me sick."

"This is a good place to be," Ruby said as if he were talking to her. The tiki torches quivered in a light breeze off the ocean. Pele, the goddess of fire, was everywhere, in the engines of the Buicks racing down Kalākaua and in the lighters men and women used to ignite their Lucky Strikes and Winstons. Ruby watched Pele dancing in the tiki torches and jumping out of the match the *haole* man at the table across the lanai was holding up to the cigarette of the plump blonde he'd picked up a half an hour before. Once when Ruby was working with her sister, Emmy, on the Big Island, Kīlauea was erupting, and she saw Pele moving in the lava as it ran down to the ocean. That was Pele at her most beautiful, the molten rock, liquid and glowing red as it raced down the mountainside.

"Where's your husband?" Richard Carstens asked, stirring the bourbon-coated ice in his empty glass with a green plastic swizzle stick.

"That bastard, did he send you?" Ruby's voice snapped like a rubber band. She couldn't get away from that man. He ruined everything. The breeze off the ocean chilled her bare arms, and the mai tai Gilbert placed before her had an oily glaze on its surface. The pineapple slice was brown around the edges, and the paper umbrella torn between two of its toothpick spokes.

"What are you talking about?" Richard Carstens stirred the drink that Gilbert had just set down in front of him. He moved his arm away from Ruby.

"He's *haole*. You're *haole*." Ruby drained her glass and signaled Gilbert for another one. She was shaking her head and tapping the middle finger of her right hand on the bartop.

Richard glanced at Ruby's empty glass. "What's *haole*?" he asked.

She closed her eyes and listened for her mother's voice. The thought of her husband was jumbling Ruby's brains, scrambling them like a big skillet of eggs on a rainy Sunday. She didn't want to find another bar. It was too late, and she didn't want to go back to her room and spend the night looking at the snow on the TV set or listening to the traffic until the sun rose. *Mom, Mom, Mom,* she chanted to herself. *He's okay,* her mother said finally, and Ruby's mind cleared like the ocean after a storm passes. She opened her eyes and smiled at Richard.

"*Haole's* the Hawaiian word for white."

Richard Carstens looked around the dim lanai. "There are *haoles* everywhere."

"You couldn't be more right about that."

"You sound as if you don't like us much."

"Maybe too much." Ruby smiled. Her mother's voice was still murmuring like a soft rain. This was the magic moment. She wasn't too drunk, but she was feeling as if she could dance on the ocean and never touch the water.

Richard was starting to feel his drinks, too, as if the bourbon were a solvent breaking down the stiffness in his shoulders and spine. "Teach me some Hawaiian words," he said to Ruby. "I want to go home with more than a sunburn and an ulcer."

"Okay," Ruby said, chewing on some ice. "*Okole.*"

"Oh-KO-lay," he said, drawing the syllables out. "What's that?"

Ruby cocked her shoulder back, slapped her own rump and laughed. "You better watch your *okole* when you leave this place, especially if you have another drink or two. There are guys who make a living rolling *haoles* from the mainland. When I dance the hula, if I don't move my *okole*, then I'm not doing it right."

"The first night of the conference, there was a luau. There were hula dancers after we ate."

"How'd you like the poi?" Ruby asked and laughed again at the face he made, like a baby with a mouthful of strained peas.

"I liked the hula," he said.

"*Haole* hula, tourist hula." Ruby spat the words out as if they were a bitter weed. "That's not the real hula."

"So what are you, a hula expert?"

"As a matter of fact I am," she said, straightening her arms and flexing her fingers. "My sister and I used to have a *hālau,* and we did shows with our best students. We were going to make a tour of Japan."

She turned on her barstool and looked out into the night. The blonde's date lit a cigarette for himself and was leaning back to tell a story, laughing at his own joke, waving his hand in the air. Ruby followed the dull red glow of the tip of the cigarette as if it were going to write a message for her in the dim light of the bar.

"What happened?" Richard Carstens asked.

"My sister died," Ruby said. "She was walking down Kālakaua to dance at the Royal Hawaiian, and a drunk in a pickup truck ran her down on the sidewalk. He killed a Japanese girl, too. She was here on her honeymoon. They said the husband wouldn't stop moaning, just sat on the sidewalk with his wife's blood all over him." Ruby focused on the blonde across the room. She was looking over the shoulder of her date, watching the palm fronds shiver in the wind. "Emmy lasted for a week in the hospital."

"My God." Richard Carstens was searching Ruby's profile, the soft curve of her nose, her full lips, the dark swell of her hair. "What happened to the truck driver?"

"He went to jail for a couple of years. He's probably out now, drinking beers and jumping sidewalks."

Gilbert put another mai tai down in front of Ruby and took the empty glass. The ice in the new drink glistened with a sheen of rum and fruit juice. The pineapple was fresh and golden, the parasol dark blue. Gilbert touched her wrist with one finger and looked at her. That meant, *Slow down, Ruby.* She nodded, took a deep breath, and counted to ten.

"Was he a *haole?*"

"Who?" she asked, exhaling.

"The man who killed your sister?"

"No, he was a local guy." Ruby sipped the drink. "Japanese, Chinese, Hawaiian, Portagee, a little bit of everything. The show was *pau* after that, finished. I'm a good dancer, but Emmy was the star. It was like all the old gods were moving inside her, especially Pele. Emmy had fire inside her, in her hands, her feet, her *okole.*"

"Emmy. That's short for Emily?"

"No, Emerald. My mother was going to name her next girl

Opal and then Sapphire. It's a good thing my dad got killed in the war. Who knows how far she would have gone. I could have had a brother named Diamond Jim Kaapuni."

"So Kaapuni isn't your married name?"

Ruby raised her glass. "You're smart for a *haole*," she said and took another dainty sip of her drink.

"What's your married name?"

Ruby narrowed her eyes. "Are you a cop?"

"Why?" Richard Carstens said. "Did you rob a bank?"

Ruby laughed. "I wish. I'm going to have to go home tomorrow, and I'm not looking forward to it."

"Why don't you get a job?" Richard Carstens was nursing his bourbon. He wasn't a big drinker. No broken veins, and all the skin around his eyes was tight. Ruby thought he was thirty-six. She was pretty good about guessing people's ages.

"Doing what?" Ruby tilted her glass, and the ice cubes did a little hula in the liquid.

"You said you could dance." He'd turned toward her and was leaning on the bar on his elbow, his head cupped in his hand.

"Dancing the *haole* hula? No thanks."

"What's a *haole* hula?"

"'Little Grass Shack,' 'Lovely Hula Hands,' 'Hukilau.' That's what I like about this bar. Gilbert doesn't play those kind of songs."

"What's *hukilau*?"

"Are you sure you're not a cop?"

"Yeah, I'm a cop. What's *hukilau*?"

"It's fishing with a net. 'The Hukilau Song' is kind of fun. The kids really like it. There are a lot of Hawaiian words in it. *Humuhumu-nukunuku-ā-puaʻa* is the name of a fish. I love those long words. They're like a dance in your mouth."

"How come you know all these Hawaiian words?"

She shrugged. "Everybody knows a few. But my *tutu*—that's my grandmother—and my mother, they're the ones who taught us. When Emmy and I were little girls, they talked Hawaiian all the time, especially when they didn't want us to know what they were saying. Emmy picked it up, and they got so excited they taught us both. You're here because of Kū, the god of war. He has about thirty different names. Kūkeolowalu is the god who makes things grow. Kupaaike'e is the god of the canoe makers. His big tongue helps eat out logs. Kuahana kills for fun. Kuahana ran over my sister in that truck on Kalākaua. Kū is making the tanks and guns for your war."

"You son of a bitch." The plump blonde woman across the room slapped the man she'd been sitting with for the last hour and ran out of the bar. Her face was red. Everyone turned to look at him, but he just sat and stared at the door as if the woman had gone to the bathroom and was coming back in a few minutes. Ruby and Richard Carstens both turned back to the bar, and Gilbert went back to washing glasses and stacking them on the drying rack.

Richard Carstens didn't want to talk about Kū anymore. It reminded him of the panel he had chaired that afternoon and the general with the gray crewcut and thick eyebrows. "Is there a god for the hula?"

"Laka's the god of the hula," said Ruby, turning in her seat and resting her back on the bar. The man across the room lit another cigarette and was staring past the palm trees that bordered the lanai of Kono's. His thin face reminded her of her husband's, the coals of his eyes smoldering in the dark. "Before you dance, you pray to Laka to guide your body. Before the hula you pray to Pele, too, for her fire." Ruby paused. "You're a funny guy. You're not like a cop at all."

"I teach political science. That's why I'm at this conference." He turned, put both elbows on the bar, and rested his forehead on his upturned hands. "No one can stop this war."

"Maybe," Ruby said. "But Kū's only one of the four big gods. Lono's strong, too. Have you ever been in a hurricane? Lono's stronger than Kū."

"But when the storm is over, what happens? People clean their yards, the roads get fixed. War never goes away."

"Kāne is the god of water and forests. He has twice as many faces as Kū."

"He'd need twenty times as many. Kū could devour the world with just one body, one face, one bag of tricks." Richard shook his head. If he were home tonight, he'd be bowling with a group of guys from work, eating burgers and shakes, talking about politics. They were all Kennedy men, but they didn't know how to think about this war. Richard's uncle had been killed on Omaha Beach, his father had been wounded in the Pacific.

"Kū is strong," said Ruby, "but not as strong as all the other gods put together."

"He's not, huh? Have you heard about Hiroshima, Nagasaki?"

"Fire," Ruby said, her voice thick with the rum she'd been drinking. "Pele's strong, but she's beautiful, too. She flirts with Kū, but she can't leave her home in Kīlauea for long. No fire lasts forever. The rains come, and Pele goes back to the Big Island."

Richard couldn't believe he was talking to this woman about religion. He went to church with his wife and sons every Sunday, but he didn't believe in God. "How many names are there for the rain?"

"Hundreds. There's a name for the rain that sweeps through the Nu'uanu Valley, and another for the kind of rain in Makiki. *Waikaloa* is the cold rain that comes to Honolulu in the wintertime. There's a hula my *tutu* taught us for the rain.

> *He ua la, he ua la,*
> *He ua pi'i mai;*
> *Noe-noe halau,*
> *Halau loa a Lono.*

She spoke in a quiet rhythmic chant, as if some other voice was moving through her like the wind in the trees or the waves slapping the sands of the beach a block away.

"It means the rain is coming. The *hālau*—the place where you dance the hula—is dark. It's a funny hula, because you do it sitting down. It's called *kōlani*. My *tutu* showed us, but only she could do it. I think you have to be at least sixty before you can even begin to think about doing this hula."

"Your *tutu* sounds like a remarkable woman," Richard said, his face now open as a plumeria blossom after a light rain.

"Oh, she was, and Emmy would have been just like her. I sometimes try to dance that day on Kalākaua—the sun, the sound of the surf, the people walking by, the trade winds, and then Kuahana running in to snatch that Japanese bride and my sister. There's a hula that you dance on the spur of the moment. That's all I can do these days. Kuahana should have taken me. I would have been happy to go with him."

Ruby slid off her bar stool and kicked her slippers to the side. It was way past midnight, and only a few people were left at the bar, and they were sitting at tables in the shadows thrown by the tikis. Ruby turned to one side and pointed her right foot and drew it back, whispering to herself with her eyes half closed. Richard Carstens had never seen anything like the movements that ran through her body.

He had come to this bar because it was scruffy, because it wasn't in a hotel, because the palm fronds that were woven into the roof over the bar were blowing off in the wind from the ocean that had suddenly become stronger with a voice that promised rain. What would the name of such a rain be, the rain that was forming around Ruby Kaapuni's hula?

Ruby was turning on one foot and tapping the floor with the other foot as she made a circle. Her legs were like the fronds of a palm, swaying in the breeze. She was wearing a knee-length shift of midnight blue, and her long dark hair fell over her shoulders like a wave in the ocean at night. After she turned, she stopped, knees bent, and she swung down low to the right and left and then up again. She clapped her hands over her head and thrust her hips from one side to the other, and it was as if all the gods had come into that flickering lanai and were moving in her body. This was not the hula he'd seen at his luau, but something darker and more violent, as if a boat had started in a calm sea but found itself engulfed in a roiling storm, the waves towering over the tiny wooden vessel, crashing down on the decks, the sailors clinging to the mast or anything else they could find. Ruby's feet stamped the floor of the bar, and she chanted, the sound coming from deep inside her body, but as suddenly as the storm had erupted it fled, and Ruby's arms again seemed to flutter in the trade winds that cooled the islands.

She turned to him and smiled. "That wasn't Kalākaua after all. That was a hula of tonight." She climbed back on the bar stool. "What time is it?"

He looked at his watch. "One-fifteen."

"Late, yeah?" She glanced back at the sky. "The clouds are moving fast. It's going to rain."

"Are there words for the clouds, too?"

"Oh, sure. At least twenty or thirty. Just like English. We're the only ones here. I think Gilbert wants to close." She opened her purse to pay for her drinks, but the big bartender waved her away.

"Not many nights I get to see a hula like that," he said, drying a glass. "See you tomorrow?"

Ruby eased herself off the stool. "I don't think so. I have to go home. I'm missing Chris and Lani."

Ruby walked out of the bar with Richard Carstens, and they strolled toward Diamond Head. The wind was picking up, whipping her hair around her head like a cyclone.

"Here's my hotel," he said.

She stopped and looked up at the tall building. "Don't let Kū scare you too much. All the other gods will keep him straight. They let him yell for a little bit, but they always pull him back."

He nodded and took her fingers in his. "Thanks for teaching me those words."

She smiled and squeezed his hand. "Don't forget to watch your *okole*," she said and turned to walk down the street.

The rain was coming now in a fine mist. What was the word for this rain? What was the word for the sky of scudding clouds with stars glittering behind? What was the word for the rumbling that was coming across the ocean from Asia, a dark drumming that no one could hear but soon would tear holes in the sky and earth? Ruby Kaapuni would know these words, would know how to talk about the war the only way it could be talked about, not with the barks of the generals but in the terrible voices of the gods, the old songs that drove canoes across the ocean or took the form of a pickup truck leaping onto a sidewalk and killing two women who were walking down the street. Richard wanted to run after Ruby and beg her to tell him all he couldn't say, but she was too far away, at the end of the block, crossing to the next one, now breaking into a little run as the rain began to come down harder, the wind blowing off the ocean, pulsing like the hand of an angry god.

Invasion
of the
Haoles
1959

Katherine Higata wrote her mother and father dozens of letters before an envelope with the postmark Springfield, Ohio, October 15, 1952, arrived at her house in Honolulu. It was addressed in her father's small spiked handwriting and smelled dry and smoky. She could picture him with an ink pen in one hand and a cigarette in the other, his thin balding forehead creased and dry as a leaf of tobacco airing in his barn. He thanked Katherine for the photographs of newborn Linda she'd sent two months before. Katherine's husband, Lester, had taken them the day they brought Linda home from the hospital. After that, Katherine's father wrote once a month. They were ordinary chatty letters about his neighbors, the church, his apple orchard, and

Katherine's mother's health, which was always robust, though she still took to her bed once a month with what she called female troubles.

They didn't come to visit until 1959, and by then Paul had been born and was five years old. Two letters arrived in the mail the week before Linda's birthday at the beginning of August. One contained a card for Linda with a dollar bill and was signed "Love Mamaw and Papaw" in Katherine's father's handwriting. In his letter he said he and her mother wanted to come to Hawai'i for the month of December. Would that suit her?

Would that suit her? She cried off and on for a couple of days. She'd reread the letter and then have to sit down and put her face in her hands. Lester and Linda followed her around like lost puppies. "I'm happy," she said to them. "I'm crying because I'm happy." Paul sat in the middle of the living room pushing a little black metal truck across the floor, making motor sounds and crashing the truck into a stack of blocks.

Katherine wrote her father the next day and told him they'd love to have them visit, but as soon as she put the letter into the mailbox, her mind began to run around like Paul when she let him drink a Coke or eat a Tootsie Roll. Where would they sleep? What would they eat? She would buy another bed for Linda's room. Linda was getting to the point where she would want to have friends spend the night, and Katherine's parents could stay there when they came. Linda could move into Paul's room, and Katherine could put Paul on a cot in her and Lester's room.

"What am I going to do with them for a month?" Katherine asked Miriam Oh the next day. Miriam was cutting Katherine's hair at Miriam's Beauty Shoppe on the corner of Beretania and McCully.

"Take them to the beach," Miriam said. "All *haoles* like to go to the beach."

"I'm a *haole*," Katherine said, though she wasn't really white anymore, her skin brown from being out in the sun so much with Linda and Paul. She had never figured out if *haole* was an insult or simply a description. She'd heard it used both ways, and when Lester said, "Come here, *haole* girl," he usually had hanky panky on his mind. Like a lot of Hawaiian words it meant different things at different times.

"Don't you like to go to the beach?" Miriam said, her mouth full of bobby pins.

"Sure, but my parents don't approve of bathing suits."

Miriam's eyes opened wide. "They're nudists?"

Katherine laughed so hard she almost choked, thinking of her mother's soft body like a big white biscuit and her skinny little father. She closed her eyes and sighed. This visit was going to be a disaster, but she wanted to see them, almost as much as she had wanted to get away from the small town in Ohio where she'd grown up.

Miriam took the hairpins out of her mouth and put her hands on her waist. Her hair was in a perfect pageboy, and a pink smock protected her clothes. "We need a strategy. What do your parents like?"

"Church and fried chicken for my mother; church and Chester-fields for my father."

"Plenty cigarettes in Hawai'i," Miriam said, putting the last roller into Katherine's hair.

In 1959, the year Hawai'i became the fiftieth state, Linda Higata turned seven. That was also the year the Monroes moved into the house across from hers on Lipona Street. She watched from her bedroom window as the green Rambler station wagon spewed forth children. She saw a girl her own age and maybe a boy about five like her brother Paul. The mother had a baby on her hip who was screaming so loud the little girl standing next to her had her hands over her ears. Linda thought she saw six children, but it was hard to tell because they were moving so fast.

Most of the time Linda's mother kept a close watch on her, but she was busy getting ready for her parents' visit. Linda had seen photographs of her *haole* grandparents, a plump woman with a thin mouth, her hair in a bun, standing next to a little, skinny man with a long-sleeved white shirt buttoned up to his neck. The only thing Linda's mother seemed happy about was that Daddy had painted the house last summer during his vacation. She sat at her sewing machine every evening after supper and made dresses for Linda, shirts for Paul, curtains, napkins, tablecloths. During the day she scrubbed the house from top to bottom.

One night Linda saw her father take her mother's hands in his and turn them over. They were as red as the hibiscus flowers on the bush outside the kitchen window. "Katherine," he said, "this has got to stop. Everything will be fine. They're coming to see us. That's a good thing, don't you think?"

Katherine shook her head. "You don't know my mother."

"Can she be worse than my mother? We live on the same street with her."

Linda could see the tears in her mother's eyes. "They're about equal."

Lester Higata took his wife's hands and kissed them. "Maybe your mother should stay with my mother. I read a book once where a character just caught on fire and burned up. Maybe they'd start a fire together."

"Oh, Lester," she said and rested her curly dark head on his shoulder. He put his arms around her and stroked her hair.

On Saturday morning after breakfast Katherine let Linda and Paul watch cartoons on the little black-and-white set in the living room. Paul was lying on the couch sucking his thumb and watching Sylvester grab Tweety Bird for the hundredth time. Linda looked out the picture window to the quiet street, which was like a television show, but everything was in color. Across the street the new family began to trickle out of the house. The mother put the baby on a blanket in the side yard. The big girl led a toddler, and the boy Paul's age with blond curls dragged a big bag followed by a smaller boy and girl who might have been twins.

Linda left the couch and stood by the window. She counted six children. The older boy and girl were putting semicircles of wire in the ground at intervals. The little boy and girl pulled what looked like giant wooden hammers out of the bag.

Linda opened the front door and sat on the steps. The boy and girl were hitting colored balls through the little hoops of wire stuck in the ground.

"Rachel," the mother called, "let Tina play," and she pushed the little girl forward. The mallet Tina held was taller than she was.

"She's too small," the older girl said, hitting her red ball through the wire.

"Teach her. How do you think you learned? I taught you."

"I want that girl to play," said Rachel, pointing to Linda, who was standing on the sidewalk now.

The mother turned to Linda. "Do you want to play?" she called across the street.

"I can't cross the street unless I ask my mother," Linda said.

"Well, go ask your mom," Rachel called, "and hurry."

Linda ran back into the house. Paul hadn't moved from the couch. He was sucking his thumb and squeezing his penis with the other hand. He always waited until the last minute to go to the bathroom. Linda found her mother in her parents' bedroom reading a letter from a box that she kept in the top of her closet. Linda stood at the door for a minute and watched her mother wiping tears from her cheeks with one of her husband's big handkerchiefs. She glanced up and saw Linda.

"It's from a high school friend who was killed in the war," she said, folding the letter and placing it back in its envelope.

"Can I go across the street?" she asked.

"May I," her mother said, standing and brushing out the folds in her cotton dress. "What's across the street?"

"The new girl asked me to play. May I go? Her mother's outside watching them."

Katherine Higata took her daughter's hand and led her into the living room. "Paul," she said, "go to the bathroom right now," and turned off the television. Paul looked up as if an alien spaceship had landed. "And come outside when you've finished."

"What's that game?" Linda asked her mother, who was peering out the plate glass window.

"Croquet," she said, wiping her eyes again and blowing her nose into the handkerchief.

The Higatas drove to Aloha Tower on December 1 to pick up Katherine's parents. She had chosen everyone's outfit and washed and pressed them the day before. Linda's scalp hurt from the tight braids her mother had put in her hair that morning, and Paul looked like a GI with his nearly shaved head.

The *Lurline* was coming into the harbor, and people were swarming the docks. Katherine ran ahead, holding her hat on her head with a gloved hand. Lester followed, holding Linda's and Paul's hands.

"There they are," Katherine said when the giant white ship pulled up to the dock. She waved, but there were so many people on the dock, it would be a miracle if her parents could see her. Lester let Linda's hand go and put his hand on Katherine's back. He could feel the sharp bones of her shoulders. She hadn't been able to eat for the last week.

"I see them," he said, recognizing them from the photos Katherine kept on her dresser in their bedroom. He pointed to them for Linda. "Your grandfather is wearing the brown suit and your grandmother the navy blue dress with the polka dot collar."

Linda looked at the mass of people and spotted the two *haoles*. They looked like some of the missionaries who came to visit their church, white with bodies that seemed uncomfortable in the sun, their clothes stiff and dark like the costumes of the paper dolls she cut from the pages of *McCall's*.

When the two older people walked down the plank, Katherine rushed over and threw her arms around both of them. Her mother stepped out of the embrace and left it to her husband, who enclosed his thin daughter in his own thin arms. Katherine was weeping now, kissing her father. She turned to her mother, who stepped back again.

"Introduce me to my grandchildren," she said over Katherine's head.

That evening after dinner, Lester Higata sat in the backyard with his father-in-law, both men smoking cigarettes in the falling light.

"Honolulu is growing so fast," Lester said. "We have to come up with a solution to the traffic problem. That's what my office is working on now. I favor a railway system instead of highways, with satellite cities in the outer parts of the island—

Wai'anae, Waipahu, Waialua, Lā'ie. People could find affordable housing in these towns and then ride the train into Honolulu for work."

"Won't that be expensive?" his father-in-law asked. He was sitting on a lawn chair, his white shirt glowing in the half-light, the end of his cigarette hovering around his face.

"Sure, but it's the best solution for the island. In the long run it will be cheaper than paving over the land. I just hope we can convince the legislature." He put his cigarette out on the bottom of his shoe and put the butt on the aluminum arm of an empty chair.

His father-in-law nodded. "I've found that most men can't be bothered to look at next week, never mind twenty years in the future."

Lester felt his heart tip like a boat in rough seas. This thin *haole* man was right. Lester could see the highways covering O'ahu like scars. All his blueprints and plans were nothing compared to the impulses that surged inside every human body like firecrackers going off for Chinese New Year. If a man could spend his last dollar on a drink while his children were hungry, how could Lester expect anyone to want to pay for a rail system that would pay for itself in thirty years, if then?

"Lester's mother is having us over for lunch after church," Katherine told her mother on Sunday morning.

"Isn't she going to church?" the older woman asked, looking at the mirror and settling her hat at an angle and then anchoring it with a pin. Linda sat on the bed staring at her grandmother. You could have put two of her mother into her grandmother's dress. Her arms were big, the upper part hanging over her elbows like white dough.

"Mama," Katherine said, "she's a Buddhist. I've told you that. She doesn't go to church with us."

"I hope you don't go with her," the older woman said, her voice like a metal zipper.

Linda thought of all the festivals they went to at the Hongwanji Mission on the Pali Highway. Her favorite was the O-bon festival.

Her Japanese grandmother had given her a special kimono to wear for the dance. Katherine didn't dance, but she got to wear a beautiful dark blue kimono with silver thread. She even worked at the *andagi* booth, making the Okinawan doughnuts and sprinkling them with sugar.

Katherine turned to Linda, "Honey, go put your shoes on. We're going to be late for Sunday School."

"This is a real Japanese meal for you," Mrs. Higata said to Mr. and Mrs. Thompson. "When you go back to the mainland, you can tell your friends." She nodded and sat down on a bright red silk-covered dining room chair that she'd turned away from the table. The silk was covered with clear plastic as was every other piece of furniture in the living room and dining room. The odor of the plastic vied with the scent of the chicken and noodles coming from the kitchen.

Mrs. Higata was so tiny that she made Katherine's father look big, but small as she was she filled the room. Lester's sister Gloria was there, too, her upper eyelids thick with eyeliner, her red lips pursed around her third cigarette.

"Linda," Mrs. Higata said, "go to the kitchen and bring in the punch for you and Paul."

"Oh, Mom," said Gloria, as Linda left the room, "already training her to be a little servant."

"It's good for her to help. I should have made you do more," Mrs. Higata said, getting up and moving toward the kitchen.

"It's a woman's place to serve," said Mrs. Thompson as if drawing breath up from her big soft bosom. "The Bible is very clear on this. A woman rules in the home, but she is servant to her husband and family. It's never too early for a girl to learn this lesson."

Mrs. Higata nodded. "You are so right. Girls today wonder why they get divorced. They don't take care of their husbands, though when you marry a Korean, what can you expect?" She disappeared through the swinging kitchen door.

Gloria rolled her eyes and looked to Katherine, but Katherine was staring at her father. This would probably be the last time she saw him. He'd never weighed more than 120 pounds, and she doubted he was that heavy now. He'd had a heart attack the year before, and all he'd eat were eggs, sunny side up with coffee and then smoke Chesterfields.

Mrs. Thompson turned to Lester, "So you fought on the American side during the war?" She looked like a roosting hen, sitting on his mother's plastic-covered couch with her hands folded over her stomach.

"Mama," Katherine said, "Lester's an American citizen. Of course, he fought in the American army."

Lester patted Katherine's hand and turned to his mother-in-law. "My company was all local boys from Hawai'i. We fought in Italy and later in France and Germany."

"They were one of the most decorated companies in the U.S. Army," Katherine said. "Lester has a Purple Heart."

"We're real proud of that, Lester," said Mr. Thompson. "I told everyone at Springfield Baptist that our Katherine's husband was a war hero." He took out a cigarette, and Gloria leaned over and lit it for him with her silver butane lighter.

"You were an enlisted man," said Mrs. Thompson. She spoke to Lester but looked over his head. His dark hair was cut short, and he was wearing a navy blue suit.

"Sergeant," said Lester, thinking about all his friends who had died, so he was left to make sergeant.

"Katherine's sister's husband was a commander in the Navy," she said, her head turning to everyone in the room as if to show them what the mother-in-law of a commander looked like.

Katherine hadn't heard from her sister Edith since her marriage. As a girl Edith had pitched a fit whenever she didn't get her way, and as an adult she'd leave a room if you didn't agree with everything she said.

"Rodney doesn't have a Purple Heart, does he?" Mr. Thompson said, his voice as sharp as a nail through the haze of cigarette smoke. His wife made a little sound like air being let out of a tire.

Lester, Gloria, and Mr. Thompson all took drags on their cigarettes, and Linda returned to the room carrying two glasses of bright red drinks with ice.

"Grandma says it's time to sit at the table," she said, and the grownups moved toward the dining room like prisoners going to their execution.

———————

The next day Lester, Mr. Thompson, Linda, and Paul were pulling into the driveway with their Christmas tree tied to the top of Lester's Studebaker when a boy ran down the sidewalk in front of the car. He was followed by a *haole* man, tall with dark hair that stood up in a thatch. The man was holding a belt, doubled up. He was standing on one side of the car and the boy was on the other side.

"Wait until I get my hands on you," the man shouted over the top of the car.

Lester opened his door. He didn't look into the back, but said loud enough for Paul and Linda to hear, "Stay in this car."

The boy was on Lester's side, a handsome *hapa-haole* boy. His hair was thick and cut like the man's. He was breathing hard and his cheek was swollen with a cut over one eye that was bleeding.

"What's going on?" Lester said, standing beside the boy.

"Mind your own business," the man said, moving toward them. He was six inches taller than Lester, and his chest was wide under his plaid shirt.

"This is my business," Lester said, pushing his glasses up the bridge of his nose. "This is my house. My children are in that car. This boy is bleeding. If you don't turn around and go home, I'm calling the police."

Linda had never heard her father's voice sound so hard, harder than koa wood or even a rock. She couldn't see the man's face, but she could see his hands snapping the belt. They were big hands, with ropy veins. One of those hands was as big as her face. On the other side of the car her father put his arm around the shoulders of the boy. Linda had seen the boy playing tetherball with Winston Nakamura. His face was right at her window, but he didn't see her, his eyes were fastened on the man with the belt.

"My wife is a nurse," Lester said. "I'm going to take this boy inside with my children, and I'm going to have her look at his face. You go home. I'll call you later."

The man stiffened, and one hand dropped to his side. His hand was level with her grandfather's face. What if he hit her father?

He was so thin; this big man could break him in two. The man didn't hit anyone, but turned and strode down the sidewalk toward University Avenue.

Lester said to the boy. "What's your name?"

"Chris," he said.

"Chris, we're going to go into my house and have my wife look at that cut." He turned to the car and bent down to the open window. "Mr. Thompson," he said to his father-in-law, "could you pull the car into the driveway?"

His father-in-law slid over into the driver's seat and put the car into first and parked it under the carport.

Lester Higata led Chris into the house with Linda and Paul following behind. It was then that Linda noticed that the big *haole* family was on their front porch across the street, and Mr. Manago and his son Ronald were standing in front of their house on the next block, and Mrs. Nakamura and her grandson Winston were in front of their house. Mrs. Nakamura came over later and said Chris could stay with her and Winston, but Chris ate dinner with the Higatas and helped them decorate their Christmas tree. He said he was nine years old, and he went to the same school Linda did, but he was in the fourth grade.

"My sister Lani is in the second grade," he said. "Do you know her?"

Linda shook her head. "She must be in Miss Oyama's class."

Chris shrugged and hung a silver ball high up on the tree.

Linda Higata and Rachel Monroe were sitting on the Higatas' front porch. Linda's hair was straight as the side of a house and dark, while Rachel's was a wild tangle of blonde curls.

"How come your hair is so curly?" Linda asked.

"My mother gives me and my sister a Toni." Rachel was picking a scab on her knee, the crusty layers flaking off in her hand, with a little knob of blood in the center of the scrape.

"What's a Toni?" Linda was trying not to look at Rachel's hands. Her nails were all bitten, and some of them were bloody.

"A permanent wave. My hair's straight." She looked up at Linda through a mass of curls.

"What's the matter with straight hair?" Linda asked.

"Nothing. My mother wants it curly. It smells bad for a week, until I wash it on Saturday. I wash it every Saturday, and my mother pincurls it for church on Sunday."

"Which church do you go to?" asked Linda.

"We don't have one yet. We go to a different church every Sunday, so my mom and dad can choose. We're not Catholic. That's not why we have so many kids."

"My mother is a nurse. She says you can have as many kids as you want. She wanted a girl and a boy, so she stopped."

"I wish my mom had stopped. My brothers are so stupid. They just run around and tear up everything."

Linda looked up the street and saw Chris and Winston Nakamura walking toward them. Linda was afraid to say anything, but she didn't want him to think she was stuck up.

"Hi, Chris," Linda called. Her voice sounded funny, as if some other girl was speaking through her mouth. His eye was better though he was still wearing a Band-Aid over the cut. Winston Nakamura lived on the next block. He was a short skinny boy with knobby knees. His hair stuck out like porcupine quills. The two boys stopped.

"Hi, Linda," Chris said. "You know Winston?"

"Hi, Winston," Linda said. "This is Rachel. She just moved in."

Both boys nodded. They were holding little paper sacks. Chris looked at his, and opened it. "We go to Takahashi Store. You want some *li hing mui?*" He handed the bag to Linda. She didn't really like *li hing mui*, it was too salty and sour for her, but she wasn't going to turn down anything Chris offered her. She took the bag and picked out one of the dried plums, salt grainy on her fingers.

"You want one, too?" he said to Rachel.

"What is it?" she asked, taking the bag from Linda.

"What? The *haole* girl never know what *li hing mui* is?" Winston said, crowing like a noisy mynah bird.

"It's dried plum," said Linda. "It's a Chinese candy. It's sweet and sour at the same time." She took a delicate bite of the little plum in her hand.

"Is it good?" Rachel asked, wrinkling her nose.

"Try it," said Winston. "Then you find out."

Rachel popped one in her mouth, but spat it out right away. "Yhewew," she said, and stuck out her tongue. "That was awful."

Winston and Chris laughed. Linda laughed, too, though she felt bad, because she didn't like them either, but she liked it that Chris and Winston were talking to them.

"I bet you never know about the *menehunes* either," said Winston.

"She just moved here from the mainland," said Linda.

"So she never know," said Winston, sitting down cross-legged in the grass in front of them. Chris sat down next to him.

"The *Menehune* are the little people," said Winston. "They're Hawaiian. They come out at night and help people finish things."

"Like elves," said Rachel, hiding her bitten nails by making two loose fists.

"I can make *Menehune* feet," Winston said. "You can trick people into thinking they real." He ran to the street and dabbed the side of his hand in a mud puddle and then ran back to the sidewalk, balled his hand into a fist, and pressed the side of his hand with the little finger on the smooth concrete.

"That's the footprint," he said, and made five little dabs of mud on the upper edge. "Those are the toes." He wiped his muddy hand on his pants.

"Wow," said Rachel. "That does look like a foot. Are you Hawaiian?"

Linda blushed because her friend was so stupid. "He's Japanese," she said. "I'm half Japanese, half *haole*. Chris is half *haole* and half Hawaiian."

"Not really half," said Chris. "My mother is half Hawaiian, half Chinese."

"I'm half English," said Rachel, "and the other half is French, Swedish, and Indian."

"No, girlie," said Winston. "You all *haole*."

"Katherine," said Mrs. Thompson after dinner one evening just before Christmas. "I have to talk to you."

They were in the kitchen, Katherine at the sink, her mother in one of the vinyl chairs at the table.

"Your father told me not to, but I have to say something." Her face was set like a mask, and she was looking at the floor.

Katherine wiped her hands on a dish towel and looked out the kitchen window at the backyard. Lester was sitting there with her father, who was talking, his right hand jabbing the air to make a point, the glow of his cigarette flying through the dim air with the movement of his hand. Lester was nodding and smiling, holding Paul in his lap, while Linda sat on another chair combing her doll's hair. Without turning to her mother, Katherine said, "If Daddy doesn't think it's a good idea, maybe you shouldn't say anything." She gripped the porcelain edge of the sink.

"Katherine, I want you to come home with us."

Katherine felt as if her back were on fire, as if the whole house were burning and if she moved the fire would jump out and devour her husband, children, and father, who was laughing now as Linda crawled into his lap.

"Katherine," her mother said. "Did you hear me?"

Katherine turned and looked at her mother sitting in the bright light of the kitchen. Who was she really? A fat, old woman who'd never left the little mining town in Kentucky where she was born until she married and moved to a small town in southern Ohio. But she was also the woman who had given birth to her, and Katherine knew this was no small gift.

"I heard you," she said.

"What do you think?"

"Mama, this is my home now. Lester has a good job, and I love Hawai'i."

"I meant for you to come with the children."

Katherine's heart was beating in her chest as if it were some wild animal trying to break through her skin. "I love Lester. He's my husband. I'm not going to leave him." She stared at her mother until the older woman looked away.

"Your father said you'd say that." She shook her head. Her mouth looked the same as it had when she was eating Mrs. Higata's Japanese lunch. "He's not white," said her mother. "You might as well be living with a colored man."

Katherine took a deep breath. "I'm married to him. We have two children. I'm not leaving him."

"'Honor thy father and mother,'" her mother said. Katherine shuddered. It was the same tone Katherine's voice took when Linda hit Paul or wanted to have a cookie before dinner.

Katherine's mother stood and walked to the door to the dining room. "I didn't raise you to be like this. If you had married David Slattery, this would have never happened."

"I didn't want to be a farmer's wife. I never could have married him. You didn't like him anyway. He was Church of Christ."

"He was white, Katherine. His people were Christians."

Katherine was glad her sister wasn't in the room. Her mother and sister Edith had always ganged up on her and Daddy.

"I never wanted you to go to college," said her mother. "It was your father who said yes, not me. And this is what it's come to. I wash my hands of the whole thing." She turned and slammed the door. Katherine could hear her heavy tread in the hall.

She stood in the kitchen for a long time, until her heart stopped beating so hard and she could breathe without a pain in her chest. She put her hands over her face. The hard skin of her palms felt cool against her hot cheeks. She turned and looked out the kitchen window. At that moment Lester glanced up at her and waved. She waved back. Paul was curled up asleep in Lester's lap. Her father was stroking Linda's head. Katherine remembered sitting on her father's lap when she was a girl. It was a bony perch. She usually jumped off after a few minutes and sat next to him. They used to listen to the Cincinnati Reds games on the radio, while her mother and sister went shopping or visited friends. In 1938 she and her father had been listening when Johnny Vander Meer pitched a no-hitter. They'd danced around the living room together and screamed and whooped. She wished she could take those hours they'd spent together and can them like a jar of preserves that she could take out in years to come. Instead she opened the screen door and walked down the steps to the backyard, the glow of a full moon lighting the plumeria trees with silver.

"There's my girl," her father said.

Lester stood and kissed Katherine on the forehead. It was a light kiss, like a feather or the touch of the trade winds. Katherine reached out for Paul, but Lester held him closer. "I'll put him to bed," he said and carried Paul into the house.

Katherine sat down in the chair that Lester had just left. She reached over and took her father's hand. "Daddy, I'm so glad to see you. Thank you for coming all this way."

He patted her hand. "I had to see my grandchildren. A photograph just isn't the same."

"Mama just said . . . ."

He tightened his grip on her hand. "Don't pay any attention to what she says. You know what she's like."

"I know what she's like," Katherine whispered. Somewhere nearby a radio was playing, and the singer's voice flew above her like little brown birds into the tropical evening. Katherine imagined all the words ever spoken hovering like smoke above their heads—her mother's sharp consonants colliding with the soft pidgin of their neighbors, the lost language of the ancient Hawaiians dancing with the screams of the sailors when the Japanese bombers attacked Pearl Harbor, and farther away the German of Hitler entwined with Winston Churchill's English. How long could a sentence stay together once it had left a person's mouth? How long could a word last before it was destroyed by rain and thunder? Katherine watched her father's words rise in the cool evening until they were lost in the riot of white flowers in the trees and beyond in the lights and noise of the city—car horns, police sirens, buses taking nurses, teachers, shopkeepers, mothers, and fathers to the houses where they would sleep through the night and wake to a day as new as the sky above them.

Katherine Higata and the Four Japanese Ladies

1952

"A Japanese man always wants a son first," said Mrs. Higata to her *haole* daughter-in-law Katherine. "My husband was so proud when Lester was born. He wanted to hold him all day. Finally I had to say, 'Go fishing. This is not a man's work.'"

Katherine Higata didn't know who hated her mother-in-law more, she or her husband, but a Japanese man respects his mother even when she makes his stomach churn. Mrs. Higata was like the fierce storms that sometimes blew out of the Pacific. The morning could be calm, trade winds blowing, palms swaying, the scent of ginger and plumeria filling the air, and then suddenly dark clouds would boil up from the ocean and lash the islands with rain and winds.

"Do you want a boy?" Katherine asked her husband after dinner that night. She pulled her nightgown tight over her protruding stomach. It was the end of March 1952, and she wasn't due until August.

Lester Higata pulled the light cotton cloth up, kneeled down and kissed the round bowl of skin and held his face to it. "I want a girl who looks just like you."

Katherine laughed. "That's not going to happen. She's going to look like you. A little Japanese girl."

"She'll have dark hair, but she's going to look like you. I'll bet you."

She slapped the top of his head and pulled him to his feet. "I'm a Christian. You know I don't gamble."

"So how come you married me?"

"That was no gamble. It was the surest thing I ever did."

Mrs. Higata had wanted Lester and Katherine to move in with her when they married. "The better to torture you, my dear," said Gloria, Lester's sister. Lester had waited seven years to marry Katherine, had gone to the mainland to college thinking that she would marry another man, so he was not going to move into his mother's house and watch her wrap herself around Katherine's neck like a snake, even though there were no snakes in Hawai'i. Mrs. Higata fumed for six months when Lester and Katherine moved into a house two blocks down on Lipona Street. She slandered Katherine to anyone who would listen, until Gloria said, "Mommy, she wanted to move to 'Aiea, but he wouldn't go that far away from you." This was not true, but Gloria knew it would make her mother happy, so she lied and continued to lie to her mother with a pleasure that never diminished, even when her mother lay dying, her face like a kabuki mask. "Don't worry, Mommy. You can never die."

In a sense this was true, because her mother never did die for Gloria Higata. Even when she married for the third time, the scratchy irascible sound of her mother's off-kilter English would erupt from her own voice box and threaten to destroy her happiness with the balding owner of Inter-Island Tours, Bill Corman, a first-class ballroom dancer with a fine baritone that he exercised on more than one occasion to mollify the remnants of Mrs. Higata residing in her daughter.

For Mrs. Higata the house two blocks away had looked like a defeat so terrible that had she been a samurai she would have been forced to cut open her own body with a sword, but after Gloria's lie she came to see it as a victory. If only Katherine would have a girl, then Mrs. Higata's prayers to the Buddha would be answered.

Helen Nakamura lived one block down from Mrs. Higata's son and his *haole* wife. She had a son, Teddy. "One son—no husband," Mrs. Higata said to Mrs. Niitani, who lived next door to her and had no children. Whenever the subject of children came up, Mrs. Niitani would turn her head *makai,* toward the ocean, as if the children were there, on boats sailing back to Japan. Mr. Niitani was an accountant for the city, a thin man with black hair that stuck straight up like a clump of unmown grass. Mrs. Niitani loved to talk, but her husband spoke only when forced to and even then in a voice so soft it was difficult to hear him. He never would have married if his father and Mrs. Niitani's father hadn't been such good friends. The two old men settled it between them and told their children. Mrs. Niitani was happy. She wanted her own kitchen. She had three sisters, and her mother's kitchen was too small for four girls.

Mrs. Niitani was Mrs. Higata's friend, but she felt sorry for Katherine Higata. Katherine was a good girl, a nurse, and she had taken to Japanese ways, learning how to make rice and noodles and tea and slipping off her shoes when she entered the house. Mrs. Higata should have been happy that her son had a good wife. Not every Japanese girl was nice. Look at Gloria Higata. She smoked cigarettes and said bad words in front of her mother. She would look right into her mother's eyes and say, "Goddamn it, Mommy, you're such a bitch." It was true, but no child should say such a thing to her own mother no matter how nasty she acted to everybody.

Helen Nakamura worked in the cafeteria at Farrington High. Every morning she would wake up at five and catch the bus a block over on Beretania. Teddy had to make his own breakfast, but he was a sunny boy and did what his mother told him to do, at least when she was around. Helen was the baker at Farrington. Everyday she made two desserts—one cake and one with fruit. She had sixteen recipes. The best was a crumb cake with brown sugar on top. She made this twice a week, also a yellow cake with chocolate frosting. This was Teddy's favorite, and she always tried to bring some home for him. He liked the apple brown betty, too. Baking took a long time, so she had to get to work early—before everyone except Mrs. Lee, the Chinese lady who was in charge of the cafeteria. Some of the ladies who worked with Helen didn't like Mrs. Lee. "She too hard," said Bertha Kim, who was in charge of the serving line. "Her face like da kine ugly fish." But Helen liked Mrs. Lee. Everything was in her big black book—recipes, schedules, vacations, demerits. On Wednesday after lunch Helen sat down with Mrs. Lee and Edith Awakuni, who was in charge of the nondessert food, and they planned the menus for the next week. It was a good place to work. Helen, Edith, and Mrs. Lee all did their jobs. There was no trouble, and Helen could go home early to work in her yard on Lipona Street.

Helen's house was painted a light green with dark green trim, and the roof had long sloping gables like a Japanese house. On the porch were three shelves where she and Teddy kept their shoes and slippers. Inside was dark and cool, because of all the trees Helen had planted—in the front yard her plumerias and in the backyard two rows of papayas. Sometimes she had so many papayas, she gave them away. She'd take them in a brown shopping bag on the bus and give them to Mrs. Lee and Edith and even Bertha Kim and her silly friend, Roberta Go. Her next-door neighbor, Mr. Manago, was someone who really loved a good papaya, so she saved the best ones for him. Teddy would shimmy up the trunks of the tree when the papayas were ripe and pluck them before they fell to the ground and split open. Every morning Helen Nakamura had a papaya for breakfast and a cup of black tea. For lunch she ate whatever they were serving at the cafeteria, and for dinner she would cook rice or noodles with vegetables and either chicken or fish. Sometimes she would walk from school to Tamashiro Market in a little shack on King Street and buy fish and then take the bus home from there. *Ahi* was her favorite, but she liked *ono*, too, and the *humuhumu* or triggerfish. She would talk to the man who worked there, and he would tell her what was fresh. He'd known her husband and understood how hard it was to raise a son on her own. Sometimes he'd give her some fish because no one was buying. He knew she didn't have much money, so he liked to give her a treat. When Teddy left home to marry the Uyehara girl, then she had more money. Actually she had plenty. Helen Nakamura knew how to save. When she died, she left her grandson, Winston, the house and $23, 000 in savings bonds. It was funny how things added up.

Gloria Higata lived with her mother until she finished college. Then she moved to a house off Wilder Street. She lived with two other girls, both *haoles*. They were all teachers at different high schools. Gloria taught English at Roosevelt, Carrie Benton taught history at Punahou, and Ruth Smith taught math at St. Andrew's Priory. When Friday rolled around, their house became the first stage of a party that lasted until Sunday evening. Carrie loved jazz and had stacks of records. They'd make martinis, smoke cigarettes, and dance on the big lanai behind their apartment. People would come, bring *puupuus* or a bottle of gin or a new Count Basie record and the party would proceed from there. Gloria's brother, Lester, loved jazz, too, and sometimes he would come with Katherine. They didn't drink, but they loved to dance, and Katherine always brought something good to eat. She made the Japanese dishes better than Gloria.

One Saturday night in 1952, Gloria was sitting next to Katherine in the living room of her apartment. She was a little tipsy, and Katherine was resting because she was five months pregnant, and her legs were beginning to swell.

"What can I do to make your mother like me?" Katherine had propped her legs on the coffee table.

Gloria lit a cigarette and pulled hard on it. "She doesn't even like her own children. Maybe if you have a boy, she'll like him. But it'll be shark love. Who'd want to have a shark in love with you? Anyway, the harder you try, the less she respects you. Act as if you don't care. I wish I could do it. That's why she was so crazy about Daddy. He ignored her ugly mouth."

"What was your father like?"

"Oh, Daddy loved to fish. You know she left him in Waialua and took us to Honolulu for school. One of his friends told me Daddy had a Hawaiian girlfriend, a young girl, and that we have a little half-Hawaiian brother."

"You're kidding," Katherine said. "Lester never said anything about this."

"Lester doesn't know. It's my little secret. When she's being especially nasty, I just think about my dad's girlfriend and their child. Let me tell you, it helps."

Mrs. Higata worked as a seamstress for a dressmaker who designed custom gowns for brides and big parties. Her hands were small, and she could finish a seam so that it looked almost as good on the backside as the front. She also did beautiful embroidery, her tiny stitches like the brushstrokes of a master painter, and she had a flare for color. She always knew what shade of blue to use and how a certain shade of green would look on a piece of yellow brocade. Her boss, Diane Sato, depended on her. Diane could make the designs and flatter the customers, but Mrs. Higata was the one who cut the patterns and basted the dresses and did the delicate finishing stitches. They worked together for almost thirty years but always addressed each other as Miss Sato and Mrs. Higata.

When Lester and Katherine married, Mrs. Higata gave her daughter-in-law her wedding dress. Of course, it wasn't one of the expensive gowns, but it was a very nice white silk suit, and every stitch was sewn by Mrs. Higata. Miss Sato had been crazy about Katherine's figure.

"Oh, Mrs. Higata, she's so slim. This is going to be stunning on her."

Katherine had been standing with the basted garment hanging

on her, the raw seams tickling her arms and neckline. Mrs. Higata was kneeling and putting pins in at the waist. It was tailored and very chic.

The dress had been Miss Sato's idea. Mrs. Higata told her that Katherine's parents weren't coming to the wedding. They didn't approve of her marrying a Japanese man, even one who'd won a Purple Heart. If that didn't make someone an American, she didn't know what did.

"I know," said Miss Sato, "let's make her wedding gown." Miss Sato was short and plump, and in her mid-fifties. She'd spent her life making dresses for rich women and their silly daughters. She thought Katherine deserved something for staying in Hawai'i and marrying Lester.

In the wedding photos, Katherine looked as if she could have stepped out of a church in Paris or New York. She had a short veil like a spray of sea foam over her dark hair, and she carried a bouquet of white orchids and tuberoses. In the wedding photos Mrs. Higata was smiling, which didn't happen very often. Gloria pointed out that her mother was smiling at Katherine's suit.

———————

When the ladies at the Baptist church found out that Katherine was pregnant, they bombarded her with bedding, clothes, advice. Without her mother, Katherine was at sea. She was a nurse, so she knew what was going to happen, but having a baby come out of your own body was different than seeing it come out of someone else's body. She was scared. Mrs. Kaneshiro could see it in Katherine's eyes. Mrs. Kaneshiro was pregnant with her eighth child, but she remembered the first. All the little aches and pains were bigger, because you didn't know what was normal. She'd been lucky because her mother had been there to help her. This poor *haole* girl had no mother, no auntie, no sister. So Mrs. Kaneshiro took Katherine Higata on as her project, not that she wasn't busy with seven girls at home and another on the way. She wasn't a Christian, but she went to the church because her two oldest girls did, and they wanted her to go, too.

Here she was almost fifty and pregnant. She told Tadashi this was the last one, but he had just smiled. What could she do with that man? She didn't want to tell Katherine that she was going to have a girl, but she was. She was carrying the baby low, and she hadn't been sick. That was a sure sign of a girl. A woman carried a boy high, and the first three months were spent eating saltines and drinking ginger ale and throwing up until you thought the baby was going to come out of your mouth next. Not that Mrs. Kaneshiro had any experience. She'd never been sick once with any of her girls, and she wasn't sick now. If Tadashi thought he was finally going to get a son, he was in for a big surprise.

"You drove?" said Mrs. Higata. "It's only two blocks." She stood on her front porch and watched Katherine maneuver out of the Studebaker. Once she had both feet on the ground, Lester pulled her up straight. She was due any day and felt as if she had eaten an entire twenty-pound sack of rice. She didn't care how much it hurt, she just wanted the baby out of her body.

Mrs. Higata had invited them for Sunday lunch. Katherine didn't know how she was going to get through it. She didn't feel like eating, bathing, or sleeping. All she could manage was lying on the couch like a beached whale.

"We don't have to go." Lester was hunched over the Sunday crossword puzzle and smoking a cigarette.

"If we don't, I won't leave this couch all day."

So there she was waddling up the sidewalk in front of her mother-in-law's house. She was really there for Gloria, who was bringing a new boyfriend to lunch. His name was Cecil Kim, a Korean, and Mrs. Higata hated Koreans more than she hated *haoles*, Chinese, Filipinos, and Hawaiians. It was an ancient animosity, as opposed to the more recent ones brought on by living in Hawai'i, which, especially after the war, was getting more and more crowded with people, who didn't know their places. Her son had married a *haole* woman, but who ever heard of a good Japanese girl dating a Korean? What if they got married? What if they had children?

"Cecil?" Katherine had said when Gloria called.

"I know, I know, but he's really nice. He teaches in the classroom right next to mine. He quotes poetry. Can you imagine? He quotes Shakespeare to me. 'Shall I compare thee to a summer's day.' I was an English major. It makes me go weak in the knees."

When Katherine was lowering herself down on Mrs. Higata's couch, Gloria and Cecil showed up. Mrs. Higata's mouth, which always looked liked a prune, now pursed even tighter, as if the prune had been sucking a lemon.

"Mom," Gloria said, "this is Cecil."

Mrs. Higata ducked her head and rushed back to the kitchen, slamming the door.

Gloria looked at Lester and Katherine. "That went better than I thought it would." Everyone laughed but Cecil.

Mrs. Niitani was the only one of the Japanese ladies on Lipona Street who didn't have a job. That was because her husband wasn't dead. I'm lucky, she said to herself as she smoothed the spread on her husband's bed. First she made the beds, and then she swept the whole house with a broom and dusted. Then she cleaned the kitchen. She loved her kitchen, the green linoleum floor and the white-and-green tiled counters. Last year they'd bought a new refrigerator and stove that gleamed like little gods in the sparkling room. Every other day Mrs. Niitani got down on her knees and scrubbed the linoleum. Tonight she was making teriyaki chicken and rice, her husband's favorite, for dinner. She took a package of chicken from the freezer compartment of the new refrigerator. No one she knew had appliances like this. She put the chicken in the sink to thaw and decided to walk up to the store for some fresh vegetables—carrots, celery, and maybe some cabbage.

She locked the front door, and walked down Lipona Street and cut over to Beretania. At the bus stop, a young Filipina woman was holding the hand of a small boy. Mrs. Niitani wished she had a little boy or girl. Sometimes her house seemed empty, especially when her husband was at work. They had three bedrooms. One of them Mrs. Niitani had turned into a sewing room. The other had been a spare room for guests until Mrs. Niitani's snoring kept her husband up one night, and he began to sleep there and never moved back.

At the store she found just what she was looking for—baby

carrots and some beautiful red cabbage. The girl at the checkout counter was chewing gum. Mrs. Niitani hadn't been allowed to chew gum in school, and she thought it should be against the rules at the market, too. She didn't like the cracking sound the girl made nor the sight of her long teeth and the wad of gum rotating around in her mouth like dirty sheets in a front-loading washer.

"Two forty-eight," the girl said, between chews.

Mrs. Niitani took out her wallet and counted out the exact change—two ones, a quarter, two dimes, and three pennies. She liked giving exact change.

On the way back home the woman and her son were gone from the bus stop. Instead there was a young couple kissing—right in the middle of the day. What would Mrs. Higata say? Mrs. Niitani didn't even want to think. She didn't know what to think about so many things. Kissing, for instance. Mr. Niitani had kissed her five times in the twenty-four years they'd been married. The first time was at their wedding. Of course, he had to then. Everyone expected it. He'd kissed her to the right of her mouth, and it had lasted for two seconds. The other four kisses were quick, too. He was a shy man, but he'd given her a good house with a beautiful kitchen all her own, the cupboards full of spices and bags of rice and cans of bamboo shoots and Spam. This was all she wanted she thought as she put the vegetables into her beautiful refrigerator full of food.

Two days after the lunch at her mother-in-law's house Katherine's water broke when she and Lester were getting ready for bed. He dropped his toothbrush in the bathroom sink and stumbled on the rug as he ran into the bedroom.

"Honey, don't speed," she said to him as they raced down Beretania. "My contractions aren't that close."

She had Linda at five-thirty the next morning. Later in the day when Gloria stopped by, she said, "Now Mom can be happy."

Katherine was still a little groggy. "I thought she wanted a boy."

Gloria snorted. "You still don't understand her, do you? A boy would have been more complicated for her. A girl is nothing."

Gloria looked around the room. "Where's Lester?"

"He's down at the nursery. He just goes down there and stares at her. I'm getting a little jealous."

Mrs. Higata came the next day with Mrs. Niitani. They were surprised to see Mrs. Nakamura there with a big vase of torch ginger from her yard. She was dressed like a man—short hair, dungarees, and a man's button-down shirt, her hands stubby and hard with work. She nodded at the other two women and smiled at Katherine. "I go now and see the baby," she said and ran down the hall.

"You know her?" Mrs. Higata asked her daughter-in-law.

"She lives near us, right by the Managos," Katherine said, taking the bunch of carnations Mrs. Niitani had brought.

"I know where she live," said Mrs. Higata. "I just didn't think she the kind person you be friends with." She sat down across from Katherine and folded her hands on her lap. "She have a boy but no father."

"Oh, he died," Katherine said, shifting herself on the bed. Mrs. Niitani bustled over and plumped up the pillow behind her. "He was a policeman. Someone shot him on Hotel Street. Teddy was only five or six when it happened."

"Sad," said Mrs. Niitani. She said a little prayer of thanks that her husband was an accountant and not a policeman. Anything could happen, but the chances of someone gunning down Mr. Niitani at his office downtown were slim. Of course, he worked down the hall from the mayor, so you never knew.

Mrs. Higata sniffed. Maybe Helen Nakamura had been married and maybe not. She didn't wear a ring. Mrs. Higata's husband had been dead for eight years, and she still wore her ring.

Mrs. Kaneshiro peeked around the door. "I just saw her. I think your husband's in love." She came into the room, and Mrs. Higata gasped. Mrs. Kaneshiro had gray in her hair, and she was six months pregnant.

"I know," she said, acknowledging Mrs. Higata's gasp. "I ask myself the same thing every day. 'What's a woman your age doing pregnant?' Forty-six. But there's only one way it happens, and I can't blame my husband too much. It's my fault, too." She laughed and sat down in the other chair, which Mrs. Niitani vacated for her. "Here," she handed Katherine a package. "I brought something for you."

"How pretty, a dress. How did you know it was going to be a girl?"

"I have seven girls, pretty soon eight. I know."

A nurse came in with the baby, Lester Higata trailing her. "Time for her feeding," she said and placed the baby in Katherine's arms.

"Do you want to hold her?" she asked her mother-in-law.

"I better not," Mrs. Higata said. "It's been a long time since I hold a baby."

"Oh, come on Mom," said Lester, taking the baby from Katherine and placing it in his mother's arms. He squatted down by his mother and stroked the mohawk of wispy black hair on his daughter's head.

"*Hapa-haole*," said his mother. The baby's mouth was like a little pink flower, and her eyes though dark were wide. "She never look Japanese at all."

"She look a little Japanese," said Mrs. Niitani.

"They change every day," said Mrs. Kaneshiro. "Take lots of pictures. You won't believe what she's going to look like next week or the week after that."

Lester took his daughter from his mother and carried her over to his wife and kissed her forehead. "If she's half as beautiful as her mother, she'll be a lucky girl."

When Mrs. Kaneshiro lost her baby, she was surprised at how sad she was. She had seven big girls, but the loss of this baby nearly drowned her like a black sea at midnight, cold and swift. She'd never lost a child, and it made her feel old, more than the gray hair in the mirror or the fact that her oldest girl was in college studying to be a teacher. Everyone was kind, but after a few weeks they forgot about the baby. Even Tadashi forgot. Only Katherine Higata remembered. She drove over to Mrs. Kaneshiro's house, put her baby on the bed, and helped Mrs. Kaneshiro clean the kitchen and go to the market. Mrs. Kaneshiro's youngest girl was in the third grade, so during the day her house was more empty than the blue sky after a hard rain. Sometimes Katherine would just stop by, and Mrs. Kaneshiro would hold the baby while Katherine drove them around in the cool roads of Tantalus and Round Top. Once they drove all the way to the North Shore and stopped at Waimea Falls for a picnic.

After two months, Mrs. Kaneshiro turned to Katherine and said, "I'm okay now."

"I know you are," she said, putting the Studebaker into second and turning from Ala Moana Boulevard into the park. It was only ten o'clock, so the beach wasn't crowded. Katherine parked the car. She carried her straw basket and the reed mats to the sand, and Mrs. Kaneshiro followed with the baby.

Sometimes Katherine had a hard time believing the life she found herself living. Nothing in the little town in Ohio where she had been born and raised prepared her for Honolulu or her husband or her little half-Japanese daughter. Linda could sit now, and Katherine reached out and the little girl grabbed at her finger and held on tight.

"She's a strong girl," said Mrs. Kaneshiro, brushing sand from the mat.

"I hope so," said Katherine. As much as she loved her baby and husband, she loved these islands, the dark green of the mountains jutting out of the blue Pacific, the fragrance of the plumeria and ginger, the trade winds blowing in from the other side of the Pacific Ocean. She loved the way people talked, the soft lilt of their voices, the pidgin and Hawaiian words that no one in her hometown would understand and the Japanese words she'd learned, so many that she often understood the insults her mother-in-law spat out at her or the verbal darts she aimed at Lester and Gloria.

She loved the food—the plate lunches, the Japanese *sushi* rolls and saimin, Korean *kim chee*, the Okinawan *andagi* that was served at the O-bon festival they went to every year with her mother-in-law at the Hongwanji Mission, the Hawaiian *poke* and *laulau* that her friends served at their parties. She thought of Linda's baby lū'au that she'd have for her first birthday and the tables loaded with *lomi* salmon, *haupia*, and *kālua* pig and the *mochi* for good luck. Every Christmas she sent cards to her old friends on the mainland that said *Mele Kalikimaka*. She never missed the snow, red noses, and the colds and flu.

Every morning she woke to the warm breezes coming off the ocean and thought, I'll never be cold again, though she'd started wearing sweaters on cool evenings in January and February, something she'd laughed at when she first arrived, but now she shivered in the cool winds and wrapped the wool close. On Saturdays she and Lester would pack a picnic and take the baby to Kapiʻolani Park or Hanauma Bay or sometimes even Haleʻiwa. The sun on her shoulders, the rough tumble of the waves, the loud laughter of the big local girls with their long thick hair—they were all magic to her. She felt as if she had stumbled into one of those carnivals traveling around the Midwest when she was girl, a show in a dark tent where a magician had transported her to this paradise, though it was her hard work in nursing school and the U.S. Army that had brought her to Hawaiʻi. From the first moment she stepped off the airplane in 1944, she knew this was the place she was meant to be with its green mountains, the sharp salt scent of the sea, and the people, so different from everyone she had grown up with in the little town of Springfield, Ohio.

They were talking about her now and would go on talking about her until they dropped dead, slipping on icy sidewalks in front of the hardware store, choking on a chicken bones, having heart attacks over an Ohio State game. And in their last moments what would they be thinking about but heaven, a place without snowdrifts or bones or hearts clogged with years of bacon grease and waiting. Even as a girl Katherine had hated to wait, to sit still. She would run to school while her sister walked, run home to help her father with his apple orchard, and the day she boarded the train in Dayton for California, she was running, too, though she didn't know it then, running to this beach, this day, her friend opening the lacquered bento box with food no one in her little hometown had ever tasted.

Lester Higata in Love 1946

Lester Higata grew up fishing on his father's boat so far out to sea that sometimes they were closer to the island of Kaua'i than the North Shore of O'ahu where they lived. Lester thought all seas must be the same blue as the Pacific, a wild color that could stand up to the blazing sun, so he was surprised when he first saw the Mediterranean. It was after Pearl Harbor when he joined the army like all the Japanese boys in Hawai'i. Though their parents had come from Japan in the early part of the century to work in the cane fields, the boys had never seen the old country. They were Americans, but they looked like the enemy. So the Army sent them to Italy. The blue of the Mediterranean was paler than the blue of the Pacific, as if the Romans and Greeks had diluted the color with the white of their bones.

Thinking of this blue, Lester smoked his seventh cigarette of the day. Or was it the eighth? The only way to find out was to count how many were left in the pack, and to do that he would have to open his eyes. He drew the smoke deep into his lungs, the smell almost masking the alcohol and disinfectant that filled the hospital ward like the ghosts of his friends who had died taking Rome. There was Jimmy Matsuda and Hank Takatami, cousin of his friend Tak, boys he had gone to school with, whose fathers had worked beside his in the cane fields. He hadn't seen Hank die. David Tamashiro told Lester how the mortar round caught him as he crawled along an embankment south of Rome. Looking inland is always a mistake. Lester's father told him to look toward the water, *makai*, and the gods of the ocean would take care of him. Sometimes during the war Lester found himself praying to the Buddha when he was sleeping in freezing mud or when the sky was exploding over him. Maybe it was the Buddha who had gotten him through the war.

The scent of the cigarette and the blue of the ocean calmed his mind, smoothed the rough waves until he could open his eyes and take in the room where he lay, a long corridor with tall windows that looked out on a blanket of green mountains. He was back in Hawai'i, lying in a bed in the army hospital, perched above Pearl Harbor in the green jungle of the Ko'olau Mountains. He lay in a ward with forty beds, twenty along each wall, every bed with a man who had some kind of wound—a missing arm, a shattered leg, or like the moaning *haole* boy with the thatch of blond curls, a mind that replayed photographs of bodies so mutilated they had been tucked at once into earthen beds, left to their final dreams in the soil of Italy or France.

He wanted to tell that boy they all saw the same movies—bloody arms flying through the bright morning, men holding the heads of friends, whose dead eyes stared into the blank sky. When Lester was a boy his father used to say to him, *The dead have many things to tell us.* Until Lester saw Jimmy Matsuda's eyes staring up at the blue Italian sky he didn't know what his father had meant. He did know the sky had nothing to tell him. It was the same blue that skimmed above his parents' wooden house in

Waialua, above the White House, above Hitler's hideaway in Berchtesgaden. Hitler and Mussolini were dead now, as was his father and so many others. Don't look, he wanted to tell the moaning soldier. Pick anything—the green wall, the whirr of the fan, the sky outside the window.

Lester smoked his cigarette close to the end, the smell sharper and the burning in his lungs like a dull fire mingling with the scent of the starched sheets. Dry with smoke, his lips kissed the dampened paper and the rough tips of his fingers like a bitter lover. He rolled a few stray bits of tobacco from his tongue to the back of his teeth. After a cigarette his mind was as clear as the water near a reef, his brain as hard as the dense coral just under the surface.

"Daydreaming again."

He opened his eyes. It was the *haole* nurse who came to change the bandage on his leg every morning. The white points of her cap nestled in chestnut curls like pale tips on the wings of a dark bird. She took the smoldering tip of the cigarette from his fingers and ground it out in the ashtray on the table next to the bed.

"You're going to burn this place down one day," she said, pulling the blanket and sheet away from his body. "How's the leg?"

"Just like yesterday—full of holes."

She stripped the dry upper layer of gauze off to reveal another layer soft with ointment, which she peeled away more slowly. The nurse's hands were the color of sand, nails clipped short. He watched her face, the angle of her cheekbones and the shadow of her lashes, as if it were a mirror that could show him what he couldn't look at himself.

She turned to face him, her blue eyes like pools reflecting the sky. "It looks a lot better. See," she turned back to the leg. "The swelling's gone down, and there's no infection."

The window across the room looked out over the top of a plumeria tree. When the trade winds were blowing, the scent of its creamy blossoms filled the room. She cleaned the places where shrapnel had pierced his leg.

"You're lucky this one didn't shatter your knee." She finished spreading the ointment and unrolled a length of gauze and cut it with scissors from her basket.

"How come I don't feel lucky?" he said to keep her next to him, to keep the scent of her skin, her starched uniform, the faint hint of perfume, gardenia maybe, the cool clipped sound of her vowels, so unlike the soft pidgin of the islands.

She stopped, her hands suspended in midsnip, and turned, eyes stormy.

"You don't feel lucky because you don't see what I see every day, boys without arms, legs, faces. Listen to him." She jerked her head toward the moaning soldier. "He'll never be okay. You're lucky whether you like it or not."

She placed the layer of dry gauze on his leg and pulled the sheet and blanket over it and smoothed and tucked them between the mattress and the metal base of the bed.

"I'll try to feel luckier," he said.

"Okay, and don't smoke so much." She smiled, took her basket, and walked down two beds where a new man lay staring at the ceiling.

At one o'clock Lester closed his eyes again and waited for the soft shuffle of his mother's shoes. It started at the end of the room like one of those big German panzers sweeping toward him, as if such a tiny woman could harm a termite.

"Still sleeping, eh?"

He kept his eyes closed. His mother's scent covered him like a blanket of nettles.

"I know you're awake, so open your eyes."

She was sitting in the hard wooden chair beside his bed, her blue-and-white cotton kimono smooth over the angles of her spare body. Her hair was caught up in a neat bun on the back of her head, two wooden sticks holding it in place. He was always surprised to see the strands of white in her hair. She was only fifty-two. Before the war her hair had been as black as the lacquer trays she'd brought with her from Japan when she'd come as a picture bride to marry his father. Now his father was gone, and around the corners of her eyes were tiny lines like the footprints of birds on wet sand. Under her small hands was a box wrapped in brown paper and twine tied in a double knot. The loops of twine at the end of the knot hovered over her hands like a dragonfly. She handed Lester the box.

"Sushi," she said, as she did every day.

He unwrapped the box and gave her the twine and brown paper, which she folded and put in the open straw bag at her feet. She looped the twine around her fingers and placed it next to the paper. On the square porcelain plate were eight cylinders of rice wrapped in thin layers of black seaweed. He lifted the plate from the box. His mother scooped up the box and handed him a bottle of shoyu.

"Eat," she said. "Fish and green onion."

His hands were shaking. He wanted another cigarette, but his mother's eyes stopped the desire in his throat like a rock. He swallowed and clamped his upper teeth to his lower lip. It felt like dull blades digging into the soft flesh but steadied his hands enough so he could pick up one of the rolls and place it in his mouth.

"I buy the fish this morning," she said.

He finished it and put another in his mouth. Her eyes never left his shaking hands.

"Good," he said, nodding at the six rolls left on the plate.

"Another Japanese lady lives on my new street," she said. "Mrs. Niitani."

He nodded, still chewing.

"Mrs. Nakamura lives there, too, but she's rough like a man. Mrs. Niitani say she never have a husband, but she have a big boy. 'Maybe he belong to a sister or brother,' say Mrs. Niitani. 'Or maybe not.'"

"Where's the house?" He asked his mother. The names of these women were crowding his brain like termites crawling on a rotten piece of wood.

"I tell you twenty times—near the university but *makai*. I'm lucky your father was such a smart man. I never want to buy insurance. I tell him it's a waste, but he is right. I move from Waialua to Honolulu, and I have my own house. Your father very smart man." She nodded her head as if bowing before a shrine to his father's intelligence.

His father was smart to take his boat out in the shining morning and be caught in a squall off the island of Kaua'i. He was smart to have broken from the cold lacquer of his wife's eyes. He was smart to be free of this world, swimming like a fish in the deep reaches of the Pacific.

"Sometimes I see Dad out in the middle of the ocean in his boat," he said, "fishing for the big ones and reeling them in."

"What you talking about? Your father is dead. Mr. Tanaka found his boat washed up on the leeward side of Kaua'i. He even sail it back. I keep for you, for when you come back from the war. How can he be alive?"

Lester pressed his hands hard against the sheets. The tremors were moving from his fingers to his arms. He needed a cigarette. His mouth, his lungs, his hands needed the discipline like a soldier needs his sergeant. He needed the sulfur flare of the match, the scent of the burning wood, the smell of the tobacco, and then the smoke rising from the leaves like incense.

"Your father's dead," she muttered, taking the half-empty plate and putting it in her straw purse. "How can he be in that boat when it stay in Mr. Tanaka's front yard waiting for you to fix it and take it fishing? Why I have such children? Your sister go to college, so now she think she smarter than her mother. She wear red lipstick and smoke cigarettes. And you talking all the time about your father being alive."

He had stopped the shaking at his elbows, the knob of bone like a dam on a storm-swollen stream that rushed down from the mountains in the center of the island.

His mother stood, clutching the handles of her bag in both hands. "I have to go. I want to tell you about my new job, but we waste our time talking rubbish."

"Don't go. Tell me," he said, his voice jumping like papaya leaves in the wind before a storm.

"I tell you tomorrow," she said and disappeared between the rows of beds.

Lester's arms exploded like the earth shattered by a bomb. He lunged for his pack of cigarettes, but his fingers sent them flying under the bed of the sleeping man beside him. Even if he had been awake, he couldn't have helped Lester. His leg was in traction.

"Where are they?"

It was the *haole* nurse. She was looking at his hands. They were trembling like wild animals trying to escape from a trap.

"Under Levine's bed."

She squatted down, her white skirt tight over her haunches.

The curve of her thighs caught Lester like a blow to the chest. His hands calmed down at once while his heart began to pound.

"I have them," she said, standing and smiling. She lit one and put it between his lips.

He closed his eyes and inhaled, the smoke washing through his body. He opened his eyes, sure she would be gone, but she stood by the bed, the light from the window shimmering around the edges of her hair. On her white uniform was a little gold pin, and two brown hairpins held her cap in place. Her neck was slender and her face was long with a strong jawline. All the pieces were good, but not beautiful. Then there were her eyes, the blue of the sky just after sundown before the reds and yellows erupt from the sea.

"Your eyes are blue," he said.

She turned her head to the side like a cat. "Yes, they are."

"Why are you following me?" Katherine asked. She was in the nurses' station loading her basket with gauze and ointment.

"The doctors tell me I should walk," Lester said, leaning his arms on his crutches while he rested his bottom on Nurse Foster's desk. He was watching the pull of the white fabric of Katherine's uniform over her breasts as she reached up for boxes of gauze from the green metal cabinet.

"They're right, and there's a beautiful garden for you to walk in. I wish I could be there instead of being cooped up inside."

"I'll tell you stories while you work."

She pushed her cart out the door and turned down the hall. "What kinds of stories?"

"What kind do you like?" He pulled himself up on the crutches and swung around beside her.

She stopped, her head at an angle as if she were thinking. "Tell me about yourself."

"Me? There's nothing to tell. Just a poor boy from Waialua."

She was moving again, but slow enough so he could keep up. "Okay, tell me why a poor boy from Waialua speaks such good English. The other local boys speak pidgin."

"Oh, I can talk like that when I want to," Lester said.

"I've heard you, but the other boys can't speak regular English."

They had turned onto the ward he used to be in, the windows open and the trade winds blowing in the scent of plumeria. He could feel the tremble working itself from his fingertips up his arm like the tremors in the foxholes outside of Monte Cassino when the big German panzers would fire. His cigarettes were in his pocket, but Katherine didn't like the smell of them, so he leaned all his body's weight on his bad leg, sending a fireball of pain up through his thigh to his torso. He wanted to scream, but the curve of her back bent over a Chinese boy stopped him, and the fire of it incinerated the tremor in his hands.

"Are you all right," she asked, her hand on his arm. "Here, sit down." She pushed a white metal chair over to where he stood. "You wait here and when I finish, we can go get a cup of coffee." She smiled and now her eyes were the dark blue of the sky from his father's boat when they were on the sea at night.

Later when they were sitting at the canteen with thick white ceramic cups of coffee, he told her how his mother was a well-educated woman in Japan. She wanted her son and daughter to go to good schools. When he started school his mother moved with him and his sister to Honolulu, and they lived with her cousin in one room in his little house in Honolulu during the school year. There were two public school systems in Hawai'i, one for the *haoles* and one for the local kids. Only a woman like his mother was able to get her children in the *haole* schools.

"It must have been hard for you," Katherine said, blowing on her coffee.

"Not really. The teachers were good. Only a couple of times did anyone say something. One day I was sick and had to go see the school nurse. I could tell she didn't want me lying on her cot. She said, 'Why don't you go to your own school?'"

"I'm sorry," Katherine said, looking down at her cup. "I know how you feel. My parents are country people, and when I went to college, everyone made fun of the way I talked. There was one boy, Jimmy Sayers, who would follow me around and say, 'I swan, if it's not that little filly from Cabbage Gap.' And this was a Christian school. It took me four years, but I left there talking like everyone else."

She smiled at Lester, and all the shakes melted out of his body. "I'll tell you what," she said, "meet me here for coffee tomorrow morning after you walk around the garden a couple of times."

They met most mornings, and Lester told her stories about Italy. About the time he and Kenny Hirata were so sick of K rations they took some grenades out to the river nearby their camp. They waited for fish to come by and then blew them out of the water. A general had requisitioned some rice, so that night they had fish and rice. All the local boys were happy, or as happy as you could be when you saw your friends being blown apart every day.

He told her about half of the men in the 100th dying taking Rome, but the brass wouldn't let them march in during the day. They'd led the liberation of Rome, and they had to march in at night. The Romans didn't know what to think. They shouted, "Cinese, cinese," as the Japanese boys marched by. Rome was the saddest place Lester had ever been. Everyone was starving. Boys were selling their sisters. They gave them everything they had—gum, candy bars, cigarettes.

"When were you wounded?" she asked after they'd been meeting a couple of weeks. It was May, and the trade winds were soft as the touch of a child's hand.

"It was an accident. I went through Italy, France, and Germany without a scratch but got the shrapnel when the Jeep ahead of me hit a mine. Two men just disappeared."

"So you were lucky again."

"I was lucky again," Lester said, not feeling lucky, because it happened right after they got to Dachau. He couldn't tell her about all those starving people in their filthy rags, pulling the raw meat off dead animals and eating it. This was something he'd never forget even if he lived to be an old man. Or the boy they took into their tent and fed for two weeks until the captain discovered him and sent him off to the refugee camp. In this war no one was lucky.

But maybe his luck was changing. When he talked to Katherine, he felt as if the war hadn't blown him to bits and put him together, all the pieces in the wrong places. It was Nurse Foster who told Lester about Katherine's boyfriend. He was waiting for Katherine in the canteen, and Nurse Foster sat down across the table from him, her mean little eyes squinting out of a face as round as a bowling ball.

When Katherine came to meet him that day she was the same—same smiles, same voice, holding her coffee cup the same way, one finger through the handle but the bowl of the cup cradled in both hands. He told her about how he'd changed his name to Lester because he loved Lester Young's sax so much. He remembered the swoop of the music that could still fill his skull when the mortar attacks stopped long enough for him to listen.

"What's your real name?" she asked.

"Hiroshi Higata," he said.

"Hiroshi," she repeated and smiled. "Not many Hiroshis in Ohio."

Late in May, they were showing *Ball of Fire* in the hospital auditorium. Gary Cooper was an egghead professor working on an encyclopedia, and Barbara Stanwyck was a gangster's moll. Lester saw Katherine with her boyfriend—he was a captain and a doctor. Lester pretended he hadn't seen her. He and Malcolm Levine were arguing about who was sexier, Stanwyck or Myrna Loy. Lester was crazy about Loy. He loved those *Thin Man* movies. Then Katherine was standing there, looking like Myrna Loy in a nurse's uniform.

"Lester, I want to introduce you to Howard," she said, glancing at the captain.

"I've heard so much about you," he said, shaking Lester's hand. His eyes were blue, but different from Katherine's, lighter and colder.

Lester was discharged a week later and went to stay at his mother's house in Mō'ili'ili. He wanted to start back at UH as soon as he could. He'd been a sophomore when he joined the army. But when he went to campus to pick up an application he ran into his old professor who told him if he was serious about studying engineering he should go to Cal Tech. By the first of July he was in California.

It was June 1950 when he saw Katherine again. He was at the Waikiki Shell for a Count Basie concert. He was with some guys from work, sitting on the grass, and saw her in the last row of seats with a Chinese guy who had a haircut like Dagwood's. During the intermission Lester followed them to the concession stand. The Chinese guy got lost in the crowd buying drinks, so Lester walked up to Katherine. "Hi," he said. "Remember. . . . ?"

"Lester," she said. "What happened to you? You didn't even say goodbye."

"I went to California to school. I'm surprised you're still here. I thought you'd be married and living back on the mainland."

"I couldn't leave Hawai'i," she said. "I haven't met anyone yet who could take me away from this place."

The Chinese guy sidled up holding two paper cups of iced soda. He handed one to Katherine, and she introduced Lester. She remembered his last name, too.

"Lester loves jazz," she said to Albert. "Albert and I are members of the same church." Albert pushed his thick glasses up his nose.

"You're not limping," Katherine said to Lester.

"No, I guess I'm lucky."

On Sunday Lester told his mother he was going to buy a paper, but he walked over to Katherine's church and sat in the back. It was a lot different than the Hongwanji Mission where his mother went. For one thing all the minister talked about was hell, which was not the Buddhist way. At the Hongwanji Mission they talked about how Jesus and Buddha were so much alike. He didn't think this *haole* minister would have agreed. His sermon was based on a passage from Isaiah: "All we like sheep have gone astray. We have turned everyone to his own way, and the Lord hath laid on him the iniquity of us all."

The "him" was Jesus, who had taken on human sins when he died on the cross, unlike the other criminals, who were being punished for stealing or murder. The Christian story was a great one. Lester had to give them that. Their leader was executed as a common criminal, but the story was God ordered him to die to save mankind. And his birth: his teenaged mother turned up pregnant, so they said God was the father. They talked some old guy into marrying her just like Janice Tengan's family talked Delbert Onaga's older brother into marrying her. But that was different, because Delbert was the father, and he was killed in Italy.

Lester was sitting in the back of the church thinking about Jesus' real father. What had happened to him? Had he been conscripted by the Romans to build their roads? Had he died or just run away? These were questions no one could answer, not even the *haole* minister who was shouting now about iniquity, about the stain we all carried in our hearts. Lester knew he was right about this. He would always carry the stain of what he had seen and done during the war.

When the service was over Lester stood outside on the sidewalk, smoking a cigarette and looking toward the ocean. He could smell the salt water, breezes from the ocean ruffling the palm fronds overhead. Katherine came out with a young Japanese woman who was wearing thick glasses. The breeze sent the two women's print skirts fluttering. They laughed and pressed the fabric to their legs.

He was going to leave when Katherine saw him. She waved and smiled, and he walked to meet her.

"Were you at the service?" she asked, grasping the thin fabric of her skirt in a bunch to the side, which emphasized her slim hips.

He nodded and put out his cigarette on the sidewalk, grinding it with the tip of his loafer.

"What did you think?" she asked, walking toward the ocean.

"It's pretty different from Buddhism," he said, walking beside her.

"You're Buddhist?" she asked, letting her skirt go. She was carrying a Bible with gilded end pages and a worn black leather cover.

"My parents are. My mother still is."

"But you're not?" Her voice tightened like a screw going into a piece of green wood.

He said a little prayer to the Buddha, knowing he would understand. "No, I'm not," he said and turned right with her on King Street.

The next Saturday, he borrowed his friend Hideki's Plymouth and took Katherine to Sacred Falls for a picnic. She was wearing a sleeveless white cotton blouse and navy blue slacks. Her dark curly hair was short and a little messy. He couldn't believe his luck. On the long drive over the Pali and along the coast to the North Shore, he told her about his job working for the department of transportation. They were planning a rail system for Honolulu and maybe one day for all of O'ahu, so they wouldn't end up like LA. She told him about her job at Queen's. She was head nurse in the intensive care unit.

When they arrived at the falls, they ate first in the field at the base of the trail. She'd made fried chicken and brownies with peppermint frosting. When they finished they lay in the sun for a while and then hiked up to the falls. The trail was slippery because it had rained the night before, and the ground was littered with split guavas, the soft pink of their flesh sweet in the sun. Lester went first and helped Katherine climb over the large stones at one turn. As they neared the falls, he could hear the water like the roar of a turbine engine.

Katherine gasped. The sheet of water was heavy because of the rain and a little brown, and the pool at its base was high. All around the dense green of the forest tangled with the edges of the pool. There was no one else there.

He unbuttoned his shirt, folded it, and placed it on one of the big rocks that lined the pool. Katherine stared at him.

"Didn't you wear your suit?" he asked. He'd told her to when he'd asked her to come with him last Sunday.

She nodded yes and unbuttoned her blouse. Her suit was white. She folded her blouse and put it next to his shirt and pants. "My mother would kill me if she could see me here. I wasn't allowed to have a swimsuit when I lived at home. I bought one when I went away to college, and my sister found it and showed it to my parents. You would have thought I'd killed someone the way they went on."

Lester dove into the pool and swam to the falls. Katherine was speaking, but he couldn't hear her for the roar of the water. She slipped off her tennis shoes and slacks and stood on the edge. She was as slim as a girl, though she must have been twenty-seven or eight. She sat on the edge of the pool and eased herself in, so she wouldn't get her hair wet, but after swimming over to Lester the spray from the falling water drenched her, and she splashed and paddled like a little girl.

He wanted to kiss her so badly that his hands were shaking, but it was too soon. Just being alone with her was like a kiss, the water like the cool touch of her lips. When they'd swum for a half hour or so, they dried off and dressed. He held her hand seven times as they made their way down the hillside, touched her waist twice guiding her over a slippery rock. The engineer in him counted, but the man felt the cool surface of her palms. He was like someone crawling through a desert and touching the first damp sand of an oasis that he'd been sure was a mirage.

Lester had gone to church eight times with Katherine, taken her to see *Sunset Boulevard* and *All about Eve* at the Kuhio Theatre, taught her to surf at Waikīkī, taken her for saimin at the stand on King Street in Kalihi, introduced her to his sister Gloria, and kissed her goodnight half a dozen times before he invited her to meet his mother.

"Have you told her about Mom?" Gloria asked. They were walking up Lipona Street, smoking after dinner. They turned left on University and walked toward the campus. This was before the freeway, when there were still houses lining the street. Kids were playing in the twilight, and the old people were sitting on their porches talking story.

"What about her?" he asked, inhaling the smoke and the sweet scent of tuberoses somewhere near.

"Lester," Gloria said. "A *haole*. Mom's going to eat her alive."

"I'll talk to her first. I'm going to marry Katherine. There's nothing she can do." But he knew Gloria was right.

"What did you say to her?" Gloria whispered. It was Sunday after lunch. Their mother had made all her special dishes—topped off with a baked fish.

"What makes you think I said anything?"

"She's a snake and she hasn't hissed all day. Come on, what did you say?"

"That I was going to marry Katherine, and if she wasn't nice, we'd move to California."

Gloria whistled. "Lester, you're a genius."

At the table Katherine and his mother were talking about how to cook the fish, about the market on Hotel Street and even better walking down to meet Henry Watanabe when his boat pulled in from a night fishing in the deep waters beyond the reef. Katherine's face was like a soft pink lantern that lit the twilight on Chinese New Year. His mother's face was a mask, mouth pulled tight as the skin over the head of a drum.

The truth was he hadn't asked Katherine to marry him. Maybe she didn't want to marry a Japanese man. Maybe she wanted children with blue eyes and blonde hair. Maybe she wanted to move back to the mainland, to live in Ohio or Kentucky or Florida. Maybe her kisses meant nothing, cool as handshakes from her thin *haole* lips.

Suddenly she looked up at him and her eyes held his for a second, widened, and it was as if the room shimmered in the heat of her glance, like a brushfire leaping up in dry grass. Then her eyes went back to his mother, voice bland and calm as if she hadn't just looked at him, as if there were no electricity in the world, no current pulsing through wires hidden in the walls of houses, arching over asphalt in streetlamps, snaking under the volcanic red clay of Honolulu like the blood moving through their bodies, so fragile that a tiny pellet could disrupt its flow but so strong it could move them through the world, to the battlefields of Europe and back again or from the farmlands of the Midwest across the water to this little street on an island in the middle of a dark blue ocean, covered by a sky so remote who knew where it might end.

COMMON HAWAIIAN, PIDGIN, AND LOCAL WORDS

Ali'i: (AH-lee-ee) Chief, king, queen, noble, royal.

Aloha: (ah-LOW-ha) Peace, love, mercy, compassion, pity; a greeting—hello and goodbye. An incredibly complex and—at the same time—simple word.

Aloha nui loa: (ah-LOW-ha NEW-ee LOW-ah) A lot of aloha. I love this as a goodbye.

The Big Island: The southernmost island in the Hawaiian chain and the largest—the island of Hawai'i.

Crack seed: A Chinese candy, usually a dried fruit that is coated with salt and sugar. *Li hing mui* is dried plum, though there is a wet form, which is juicier than the dried. It has become a generic term that includes many dried treats not containing seeds, such as dried lemon peel and a gooey shredded mango.

Da kine: Pidgin for *the kind*. It is used in the same way standard English speakers use "the thing" or "it." *Give me da kine.*

Ewa: (EH-vah) west. In the direction of 'Ewa Beach, a town far west of Honolulu.

Heiau: (HAY-ow) Temple. There are many *heiau* left in Hawai'i. They are elevated outdoor structures made of stones with huts for the *kahuna* or priests. Heiau is singular and plural.

Hālau: School for hula.

Haole: (HOW-lee) A Caucasian person.

Hapa-haole: (HAH-pah) *Hapa* means part, so *hapa-haole* is someone who is part white and part something else—Japanese, Chinese, Hawaiian, Samoan, etc., or any combination. It's Hawai'i, so anything goes.

Holokū: (HO-low-koo) A long dress that is fitted (unlike the muumuu) with a train. It is more elegant than the muumuu and is often worn for special occasions. It makes a great wedding gown.

Howzit: (How-zit) Pidgin for How is it or Hello.

Hukilau: (HOO-key-lau) To fish with a net.

Imu: (EE-moo) An underground oven. The pig for a lū'au is roasted in an *imu*.

Ka'ala: (ka-AH-la) The highest mountain on O'ahu. It overlooks Wai'anae and Mākaha.

Kahuna: (ka-WHO-nah) Priest. Kahuna is plural and singular.

Kanaloa: (kah-nah-LOW-ah) One of the four great gods along with Kū, Lono, and Kāne. He is in charge of the infernal world and is the god of mischief, the sea, and healing.

Kāne: (KAH-neh) The god of creation, sunlight, fresh water, and forests. He is an architect and builder and one of the four great gods.

Kapakahi: (kah-puh-KAI) Messed up.

Kapu: (KAH-poo) The Hawaiian system of taboo.

Kaukau: (COW-cow) Food.

Kuleana: (koo-lee-AH-nah) Responsibility. *That's not my kuleana.*

Kū: (KOO) The Hawaiian god of war, medicine, and the male principle of regeneration. One of four primary gods in Hawaiian theology.

Laka: (LAH-kah) God of the hula.

Lanai: (lah-NIGH) A porch or veranda.

Leeward: The dry side of the island. Honolulu is on the leeward side of O'ahu.

Lei: (LAY) A garland of flowers, shells, leaves, feathers that is worn around the neck. Leis are given in greeting but also on important and not-so-important occasions. Graduation is a big leigiving occasion.

Li hing mui: (lee hee MOY-ee) Dried plums. See Crack seeds.

Lono: (LOW-noh) One of the four great gods. He rules agriculture, fertility, wind, and clouds.

Lū'au: (LOO-ahw) A Hawai'ian feast.

Māhū: (MAH-hoo) Homosexual.

Makai: (ma-KAI) Toward the ocean. This word and *mauka* are used instead of north, south, east, west to give directions. Other directions are diamond head and ewa—toward Diamond Head or Ewa Beach on O'ahu.

Make: (MOCK-eh) Dead.

Mauka: (MAO-kah) Toward the mountains.

Malasada: (mal-a-SAH-da) Portugese doughnut with no hole. The best are at Leonard's.

Manini: (mah-NEE-nee) Small or stingy.

Mele: (MEH-lay) Song, poem, chant.

Mele Kalikimaka: (MEH-lay ka-lee-key-MAH-ka) Merry Christmas.

Menehune: (men-uh-WHO-nay) A legendary race of small people who worked at night to build roads, fishponds, heiau.

Mochi: (MOH-chee) A steamed rice cake.

Moke: (MOKE) A tough local boy. Not a term that one would use and expect to escape without bruises and a black eye.

Musubi: (MOO-sue-bee) A rice ball wrapped in black seaweed and sometimes with a sour preserved red plum at its center.

Muumuu: (MOO-moo) A loose-fitting local dress that was adapted from missionary nightgowns to cover the naked Hawaiian women.

Obāsan: (OH-bah-san) Japanese for grandmother.

'Ohana: (oh-HAH-nah) Family and also acting as family.

Okole: (oh-KOH-lay) Bottom, rump, buttocks. *Move your okole. The mayor was trying to cover his okole.*

Ono: (OH-no) Delicious. *Man, Carleen's pupus are ono.*

Pakalolo: (pah-kah-LOH-loh) Marijuana. It comes from the Hawaiian words for tobacco (paka) and crazy (lōlō).

Pau: (POW) Finished, done, over. *Tracy and Donnie are pau. The job is pau. The movie is pau.*

Pele: (PEH-lay) Hawaiian goddess of the volcano.

Plate lunch: A local staple consisting of one or two scoops white rice, one scoop macaroni salad, and meat, such as teriyaki chicken or garlic shrimp or Spam, another island staple.

Plumeria: Frangipani. A tree with a five-petaled fragrant blossom that is used to make leis. They are most often white with a yellow throat, but there are many pink varieties as well.

Poi: A paste or pudding of taro pounded and thinned with water. It was one of the staples of the Hawaiian diet. The remains of the ancient taro fields can be found and some are being revived. Although poi is an acquired taste, taro chips are ono.

Portagee: Portuguese or of Portuguese extraction.

Puka: (POOH-kah) Hole. *His pants get one puka in the okole.*

Pupus: (POOH-poohs) Local hors d'oeuvres. *Sushi makes great pupus.*

Saimin: (sigh-MIN) A local noodle soup with a garnish of vegetables, meat, seaweed, really anything you want. In Pearl City, Shiro's Hula Hula Saimin Haven offers sixty different combinations to add to the basic noodles and broth. This is such a basic dish in the islands that McDonald's sells saimin.

Shave ice: Sno-cones.

Shishi: (SHE-she) Japanese for pee pee.

Shoyu: (SHOW-you) Soy sauce.

Small kid time: When you were a small kid, the past. *I went know Wendell and his sister since small kid time.*

Stink eye: Dirty look, as in: *She give me the stink eye.*

Talk story: Talk, gossip, shoot the breeze.

Tutu: (TOO-too) Grandmother or grandfather.

Wahine: (wah-HEE-nee) Girl or woman.

Windward: The wet side of the island. Kāne'ohe is on the windward side of O'ahu. Every island has a windward and leeward side. The winds and rains coming from the west hit the windward side and are stopped by the mountains. This side is always more rainy and thus more lush and green than the leeward side.

THE FOLLOWING BOOKS SHAPED MY VIEW OF HAWAI'I

Beckwith, Martha, *Hawaiian Mythology,* University of Hawai'i Press, Honolulu, 1970.

Chang, Thelma, *I Can Never Forget: Men of the 100th/442nd,* Sigi Productions, Inc., Honolulu, 1991.

Emerson, Nathaniel B., *Unwritten Literature of Hawaii: The Sacred Songs of the Hula,* Charles E. Tuttle, Co., Tokyo, 1965.

Hawaii Nikkei History Editorial Board, *Japanese Eyes, American Heart: Personal Reflections of Hawaii's World War II Nisei Soldiers,* Tendai Educational Foundation, Honolulu, 1998.

Kamakau, Samuel Manaiakalani, *Ka Po'e Kahiko: The People of Old,* Bishop Museum Press, Honolulu, 1964.

Kent, Harold Winfield,*Treasury of Hawaiian Words in One Hundred and One Categories,* Masonic Public Library of Hawai'i, Honolulu, 1993.

Pukui, Mary Kwena and Samuel H. Elbert, and Esther T. Mookini, *The Pocket Hawaiian Dictionary,* University of Hawai'i Press, Honolulu, 1975.

Saiki, Patsy Sumie, *Early Japanese Immigrants in Hawaii*, Japanese Cultural Center of Hawaiʻi, Honolulu, 1993.

Saiki, Patsy Sumie, *Japanese Women in Hawaii: The First 100 Years*, Kisaku, Inc., Honolulu, 1985.

Simonson, Douglas, and Ken Sakata, and Pat Sasaki, *Pidgin to Da Max*, The Best Press, Honolulu, 1981.

Tonouchi, Lee A., *Da Kine Dictionary*, Bess Press, Honolulu, 2005.

Trask, Haunani-Kay, *From a Native Daughter*, University of Hawaiʻi Press, Honolulu, 1993.

Donald Anderson
Fire Road
Dianne Benedict
Shiny Objects
David Borofka
Hints of His Mortality
Robert Boswell
Dancing in the Movies
Mark Brazaitis
The River of Lost Voices:
Stories from Guatemala
Jack Cady
The Burning and Other
Stories
Pat Carr
The Women in the Mirror
Kathryn Chetkovich
Friendly Fire
Cyrus Colter
The Beach Umbrella
Jennine Capó Crucet
How to Leave Hialeah
Jennifer S. Davis
Her Kind of Want
Janet Desaulniers
What You've Been Missing
Sharon Dilworth
The Long White
Susan M. Dodd
Old Wives' Tales
Merrill Feitell
Here Beneath
Low-Flying Planes
James Fetler
Impossible Appetites
Starkey Flythe, Jr.
Lent: The Slow Fast
Sohrab Homi Fracis
Ticket to Minto: Stories of
India and America
H. E. Francis
The Itinerary of Beggars

Abby Frucht
Fruit of the Month
Tereze Glück
May You Live in Interesting
Times
Ivy Goodman
Heart Failure
Barbara Hamby
Lester Higata's 20th Century
Ann Harleman
Happiness
Elizabeth Harris
The Ant Generator
Ryan Harty
Bring Me Your Saddest
Arizona
Mary Hedin
Fly Away Home
Beth Helms
American Wives
Jim Henry
Thank You for Being
Concerned and Sensitive
Lisa Lenzo
Within the Lighted City
Kathryn Ma
All That Work and
Still No Boys
Renée Manfredi
Where Love Leaves Us
Susan Onthank Mates
The Good Doctor
John McNally
Troublemakers
Molly McNett
One Dog Happy
Kevin Moffett
Permanent Visitors
Lee B. Montgomery
Whose World Is This?
Rod Val Moore
Igloo among Palms